PENGUIN BOOKS

THE LAST FRIEND

Winner of the 1994 Prix Maghreb, Tahar Ben Jelloun was born in 1944 in Fez, Morocco, and emigrated to France in 1961. A novelist, essayist, critic, and poet, he is a regular contributor to *Le Monde*, *La Répubblica*, *El País*, and *Panorama*. His novels include *The Sacred Night*, which received the Prix Goncourt in 1987, *Corruption*, and *This Blinding Absence of Light*, which won the IMPAC Dublin Literary Award.

To request Penguin Readers Guides by mail (while supplies last), please call (800) 778-6425 or e-mail reading@us.penguingroup.com. To access Penguin Readers Guides online, visit our Web site at www.penguin.com.

The Last Friend

A Novel

TAHAR BEN JELLOUN

Translated from the French
by Kevin Michel Capé and Hazel Rowley

PENGUIN BOOKS

PENGUIN BOOKS

Published by the Penguin Group

Penguin Group (USA) Inc., 375 Hudson Street, New York, New York 10014, U.S.A.
Penguin Group (Canada), 90 Eglinton Avenue East, Suite 700, Toronto, Ontario, Canada
M4P 2Y3 (a division of Pearson Penguin Canada Inc.) • Penguin Books Ltd, 80 Strand,
London WC2R 0RL, England • Penguin Ireland, 25 St Stephen's Green, Dublin 2, Ireland
(a division of Penguin Books Ltd) • Penguin Group (Australia), 250 Camberwell Road,
Camberwell, Victoria 3124, Australia (a division of Pearson Australia Group Pty Ltd) •
Penguin Books India Pvt Ltd, 11 Community Centre, Panchsheel Park, New Delhi – 110
017, India • Penguin Group (NZ), cnr Airborne and Rosedale Roads, Albany, Auckland
1310, New Zealand (a division of Pearson New Zealand Ltd) • Penguin Books (South
Africa) (Pty) Ltd, 24 Sturdee Avenue, Rosebank, Johannesburg 2196, South Africa

Penguin Books Ltd, Registered Offices: 80 Strand, London WC2R 0RL, England

First published in the United States of America by The Free Press 2006
Published in Penguin Books 2007

1 3 5 7 9 10 8 6 4 2

Copyright © Editions de Seuil, 2004
Translation © The New Press, 2006
All rights reserved

Translated by Kevin Michel Capé and Hazel Rowley

Originally published as *Le dernier ami* by Editions de Seuil, Paris

Published with the generous support of the Florence Gould Foundation.

THE LIBRARY OF CONGRESS HAS CATALOGED THE HARDCOVER EDITION AS FOLLOWS:
Ben Jelloun, Tahar, 1944–
[Dernier ami. English]
The last friend / Tahar Ben Jelloun ; translated from the French
by Kevin Michel Capé and Hazel Rowley.
p. cm.
ISBN 1-59558-008-5 (hc.)
ISBN 978-0-14-303848-1 (pbk.)
I. Capé, Kevin Michel. II. Rowley, Hazel. III. Title.
PQ3989.2.J4D4713 2006
843'.914—dc22   2005052274

Printed in the United States of America

Except in the United States of America, this book is sold subject to the condition that it
shall not, by way of trade or otherwise, be lent, resold, hired out, or otherwise circulated
without the publisher's prior consent in any form of binding or cover other than that in
which it is published and without a similar condition including this condition being imposed on the subsequent purchaser.

The scanning, uploading and distribution of this book via the Internet or via any other
means without the permission of the publisher is illegal and punishable by law. Please pur-
chase only authorized electronic editions, and do not participate in or encourage electronic
piracy of copyrighted materials. Your support of the author's rights is appreciated.

The Last Friend

Prologue

I RECEIVED A LETTER this morning. A recycled envelope. The postmark and date were hard to make out over the stamp of King Hassan II in his white jellaba. I recognized Mamed's uneven handwriting. In the top left-hand corner, "personal" was underlined twice. Inside was a yellowish sheet of paper. A few lines, harsh, dry, final. I read them over and over. It wasn't a hoax, or some kind of bad joke. It was a letter intended to destroy me. The signature was my friend Mamed's. There was no doubt about it. Mamed, my last friend.

I

Ali

I

MAMED ALWAYS USED TO SAY, "Words don't lie. Men lie. I'm like words." He would laugh at his own joke, pull a cigarette from his pocket, and slip into the boys' bathroom for a secret smoke. It was his first of the day, and he relished it. We would wait for him, on the lookout for the principal, Monsieur Briançon. We were afraid of him; he was strict and unyielding, as ready to give detention to his own two children as to any unruly students.

Monsieur Briançon was not likely to become any more lenient, especially after his oldest son was drafted for military service in Algeria. This was 1960. Algeria was already in the throes of war. Once in a while, Monsieur Briançon would talk with Monsieur Hakim, our Arabic teacher, who also had a son in the army—on the other side, fighting with the Algerian National Liberation Front. The two must have talked about the horror and ultimate absurdity of the war—and about the indomitable spirit of the Algerians, determined to recover their independence from French colonial rule.

Mamed was short, with close-cropped hair and an intelligent face revealing his wry sense of humor. He had a complex about his small, skinny physique, convinced that girls wouldn't pay attention to him until he spoke. He charmed them with his gift for language, made them laugh—but he was just as capable of making cruel remarks. He was always ready for a fight, so other boys rarely provoked him. We became friends when he came to my defense against Arzou and Apache, two delinquents who had been thrown out of school for theft and assault. One day they were waiting for me just outside the school, trying to bait me, chanting: "The kid from Fez is a swine! He's a Jew!"

In those days, people in Tangier who had immigrated from Fez were undeniably discriminated against. They were known as "the insular people." Tangier still had the prestigious status of an international city, and its citizens considered themselves privileged. Mamed stood between me and the two bullies; he made it clear that he was ready and willing to fight to protect his friend. Arzou and Apache backed off. "We were just kidding," Arzou said. "We don't have anything against you pale-skins from Fez. Like the Jews. We don't have anything against them, but they always seem so successful. Come on, we were just kidding . . ."

Mamed said I was too white and told me to go to the beach

to get a tan. He added that he, too, thought people from Fez had the same traits as the Jews, but he admired them, even though he was a little jealous of their special minority status in the city. He said people from Fez, just like the Jews, were calculating and tight with their money, intelligent, often brilliant; he wished he could be that thrifty. One day, he showed me an article claiming that more than half the population of Fez was of Jewish descent. The proof, Mamed said with a laugh, is that all family names starting with "Ben" were Jewish. They were Jews from Andalusia who had converted to Islam. "Think how lucky you are," he said. "You're Jewish without having to wear a yarmulke. You have their mentality, their intelligence, but you're a real Muslim, like me. You win on both counts, and you're not harassed the way the Jews are. Of course people are jealous of you. But you're my friend. You just need to change the way you dress, and be a little less cheap."

Seen from Tangier, Fez appeared to be a city beyond the reach of time—or more precisely, a city rooted and stuck in the tenth century. Nothing, absolutely nothing, had changed since the day it was built. Its beauty lay in its relationship to time. I realized that I had left behind an ancient era. After a single day's journey I found myself in the twentieth century, with dazzling lights, paved streets, and cars—a cosmopolitan society with several languages and currencies.

Mamed made fun of me, telling his friends I was a relic from prehistoric times. He went on and on about the tradi-

tions of old Fez, a city that had always resisted moderniza-
tion, implying that Tangier was far superior to "that old
place" so admired by tourists. Mamed's father, intelligent
and cultured, was a prominent citizen with friends in the
British consulate. He corrected his son. "Fez is not just any
old city. It's the cradle of our civilization. When our Jewish
and Muslim ancestors were expelled from Spain by Queen
Isabella, they took refuge in Fez. The first great Muslim university, the Qarawiyyan, was built in Fez—by a woman, no
less, a rich woman from the Tunisian holy city of Kairouan.
Fez is a living museum, and should be considered part of our
universal heritage. I know, our treasures aren't so well preserved, but there's no city in the world like it, and for that
alone, it deserves respect."

I liked this refined, elegant man. He would lend me books,
asking me to pass them along to his son, who had never cared
much for reading.

Mamed's house was just a few steps from the school. Mine
was on the other side of the city, in the Marshane district
overlooking the sea, more than twenty minutes away on foot.
He used to invite me to his parents' for afternoon tea. The
bread came from Pepe's, a Spanish bakery, and I thought it
was delicious. At home, my mother made the bread herself,
and it was clearly inferior. Mamed, though, preferred my
mother's bread to Pepe's. "That's real bread," he'd say to me.
"You don't get it. It's homemade. That's the best!"

2

OUR FRIENDSHIP TOOK a while to develop. When you're fifteen, feelings fluctuate. In those days, we were more interested in love than friendship. We all had girls on the brain. All of us, that is, except Mamed. He thought courting girls was a waste of time, and never went to the surprise parties held by the French students. He was afraid that girls would refuse to dance with him because he was short, or not attractive enough, or because he was an Arab. He had good reason to think this. At a birthday party for one of his cousins whose mother was French, a pretty girl had rudely rejected him. "Not you, you're too short and not good looking!" This off-hand comment took on exaggerated proportions.

Now all our discussions at recess revolved around France's war in Algeria, colonialism, and racism. Mamed didn't joke anymore. Naturally, I took his side, and agreed with everything he said. Our philosophy teacher read to us from Frantz

Fanon's new book, *The Wretched of the Earth,* and we spent hours discussing it. At the time, we all sided with Sartre rather than Camus because Camus had written: "Between my mother and justice, I choose my mother." Already very engaged in politics, Mamed said he was reading Marx and Lenin. I wasn't interested, even though I was fiercely anticolonialist. I read poetry, classical and modern.

Mamed became a militant. I fell in love, which bothered him. Her name was Zina; she was dark and sensuous. For the first time, it occurred to me that he might be jealous of me.

When I confided in him, he teased me. I made light of it. But deep down, I knew he didn't like this intrusion into our friendship. For him, it was a waste of time and energy. He readily admitted that he "beat his straw" every day. He used the Spanish word for straw, *paja,* to mean masturbation, and joked about this with his friends. The girls were embarrassed, and hid their faces, laughing. Mamed took the joke one step further, referring to girls as "exquisite straws."

Our group picnics became a time to get even. Mamed wanted to play "the defect game," as he called it, which involved each of us enumerating our flaws, one after the other, especially private, secret ones. He started with himself to show us. "I'm short, ugly, hard to get along with, cheap, and lazy. If I'm bored at dinner, I fart. You can't take me anywhere. I lie more often than I tell the truth. I don't like people and I like to be mean. Now it's your turn!" He looked at me defiantly. I launched into self-criticism by exaggerating some of my personality traits, which pleased him. My girlfriend didn't like this game, and threatened not to come out with us any more. Mamed silenced her by threatening to reveal secrets he claimed to know about her. This upset me. He told me later this was a good tactic because everyone has secrets they don't want revealed.

The girls liked him, actually. Khadija told everyone she liked him, even when he wasn't talking. We were all relieved to hear this. If Mamed had a girlfriend, maybe he wouldn't be so mean. He wasn't in love, but he saw Khadija on a fairly regular basis.

One day, we were having a picnic and everything was going fine when Mamed suggested we play the defect game again. This time, you had to list the faults of the person you knew best. Poor Khadija turned pale. Mamed started talking about the number twelve. Khadija apparently had twelve flaws that would make any man run in the other direction, and others that would turn him into a woman-hater forever. It was impossible to stop him. We protested, but he was off and running. We were scared, he said. We were cowards. Zina turned up her radio as loud as it would go to drown out his cruel words. Dalida, the Franco-Egyptian singer, was singing "Bambino." Mamed, furious, grabbed the radio and threw it in the water.

"You should listen to me," he said. "We're here for the

truth. Why should we encourage the social hypocrisy para-lyzing this country? Yes, Khadija has twelve faults. She has at least as many as the rest of us, so what are you all afraid of? She's eighteen and still a virgin. She prefers to be sodomized rather than to spread her legs. She'll suck but she won't swal-low. She wears deodorant instead of washing. When she comes, she screams the names of the prophets. She sneaks al-cohol. When she doesn't have a boyfriend, she sticks candles up her ass."

Khadija fled, followed by two of the other girls. We joined them, leaving Mamed to enumerate his girlfriend's "flaws" by himself. We were appalled, and vowed never to have another gathering on the Old Mountain again with that monster.

That night, Mamed rang my doorbell. He was in tears. He'd been smoking marijuana, he said, and drinking strong Spanish beer. Would I ever be able to forgive him?

I suddenly saw in him an unhappy young man, profoundly ill at ease, who disliked himself and everyone else, too. He needed psychiatric help. He wanted to try some kind of ther-apy, but he didn't want people to think he was crazy. He avoided Khadija completely, and generally kept to himself. I was the only person he would see. He trusted me, and made every effort to temper his mean streak. He retained his sense of irony, but used it more wisely. When I ran into logistical problems with my girlfriend—there was nowhere for us to be alone—Mamed told me about the secret affair he was having with a young woman who worked for his parents. He was "beating his straw" less and less, but was afraid his mother might send the girl away. "She's working-class," he told me. "A virgin, of course. We don't speak. I see her at night, and she waits for me naked, ass up. I lie on top of her, spread her ass, and penetrate her, with my hand over her mouth so she can't make any noise. I never ejaculate inside her. I come. She comes. Everyone's happy. In the morning, when she sees me, she looks away, and so do I."

3

DURING OUR SENIOR YEAR, when we were preparing for the baccalaureate, Mamed was more subdued. A small group of us studied together at the Café Hafa, and he would join us. He was good at math, which was useful for the rest of us. He sometimes made jokes, but was careful not to go too far. I managed to get him back together with Khadija, with whom he was now in love although he wouldn't admit it. Mamed found me a place where I could finally make love with Zina. "The frantic sessions in the cemetery are over," he said. "From now on, you can use François' apartment." Our gym teacher had gone home to Brittany on vacation, leaving the keys with Mamed, who would water the plants and feed the cats in return.

I was ecstatic. Mamed and I worked out a schedule: he used the apartment one day, I used it the next. A red thumbtack on the door meant "do not disturb." When we left, we replaced it with a green one. The summer was great. We met in the evenings to exchange confidences. The apartment was our secret. None of our other friends knew about it. Neither one of us said a word to anyone. At stake were the lives of girls who were supposed to save their virginity for marriage no matter what. We saw the girls in the afternoon, never at night. With Zina, I used what we called at that time "the stroke of the paintbrush." I rubbed my cock against her vagina without penetrating her. I had to be extremely careful. Mamed told me he preferred sodomy.

The summer of 1962 marked our relationship in a way we would never forget. Friendship begins with sharing secrets. Mamed's sister became friends with Khadija and Zina. With her as our chaperone, it was easier for us to go out. Our parents no longer had to worry about us. Mamed and I developed a code to communicate without arousing suspicion. He would say, "Tomorrow I have to water Monsieur François's plants. The next day, it's your turn to feed the cats. Don't forget to stop at the fish market for some sardines. These cats are really spoiled."

Although we weren't getting much sexual experience, we were having a good time. One day, Mamed told me he was tired of fucking Khadija in the ass. He wanted to penetrate a vagina, a real one, without guilt or fear. For that, we would need prostitutes. The best place, he informed me, was Ceuta, a Spanish enclave east of Tangier. Spanish prostitutes were known to be clean and expert. Our friend Ramon would guide us. He knew where to go. All we had to do was find the money. Mamed would tell his parents he was going to buy records, since there was not much music in the market in Tangier. His father was a music lover. Mamed would get the money by promising his father the latest recording of Mozart's *Don Giovanni.* Somehow I had to find a way to get some money from my parents.

Ramon was not one of our friends from school. He had a job, working in his father's plumbing business. We practiced our Spanish with him, but mostly we went to parties to-gether. Ramon was very popular with the girls. He made us laugh because whenever something excited him—especially the sight of a beautiful girl—he stuttered.

So there we were, on the bus heading for Tetouan, then Ceuta. We arrived in the evening. Ramon had the address of a boarding house where we could sleep, and another where we could fuck.

I drank wine for the first time, and thought it was disgust-ing. At the Fuentes Pension, the girls were sitting downstairs, their bodies on display. You had to pay in advance, fifty pese-tas a shot. Mamed chose a blonde with big breasts. In fact, she was a Moroccan with dyed hair. Ramon was a regular. He had his usual girl, a redhead with short hair and flashing eyes.

I went upstairs with a slender brunette with a sad look. I thought she was going to be an expert. She was tired and blasé. I came quickly. She heaved a sigh of relief. She washed herself in front of me, and then, when she rinsed her mouth, she took out her dentures. I went downstairs, repelled by the whole thing, and waited for the others outside. Mamed had found a good one; half an hour of fucking, as opposed to my miserable five minutes. His was named Katy. Mine was Mercedes, and I was her fourteenth client of the day. She told me her limit was fifteen. It was a matter of principle. But, she told me, I only counted for half. "You're too young for this!"

Half a client! I was upset, but didn't want to tell Mamed, who looked very pleased with himself. He told me he was satisfied, he felt good, and Katy had promised to see him in Tangier. She had a place there where they could have sex. If I liked, she would bring Mercedes. We could all go to Ramon's house. Ramon nodded in agreement.

No way! I didn't want to hear any more about Ceuta and its whores. I have never forgotten old Mercedes and her false teeth. Burlesque images replayed themselves in my mind. All I could think about was the story of the vagina with sharp teeth. Mamed could tell I was unhappy. He thought it had to do with morality, guilt, or sin. No, I was troubled because I had seen something I should not have had to see, a moment of incredible pathos: a toothless woman wiping her thighs with an old wet rag while I pulled on my pants. Mamed tried to console me. He came home with me, and we spent the evening listening to the radio. I felt like crying. Early the next morning, we went to the hammam in the Rue Ouad Ahardane.

4

MAMED NO LONGER HID when he had a cigarette, but he never dared smoke in front of his parents. It was a matter of respect. His father was a courteous, reserved man. When I greeted him, I kissed his hand, as I did with my own father. He did not know that everyone called his son Mamed, a diminutive of Mohammed.

One day, a school friend phoned Mamed's house, and his father answered. He did not appreciate his son's nickname, and gave him a lecture. "It was an honor for me to give you the name of our beloved prophet. I slaughtered the sheep with my own hands at your baptism, and here you are allowing yourself to be given this ridiculous name. Your name is Mohammed, and I don't want to hear 'Mamed' ever again."

Mamed told us about this, adding that he was a bad Muslim, and found it difficult to bear the name of the prophet.

Anyway, practically everyone in Morocco was named Mohammed.

During the month of Ramadan, when Muslims are supposed to fast between dawn and dusk, we went to see our
friend François. He had prepared mushroom omelettes for
us. Mamed insisted on having a slice of ham and a glass of
wine, too. Not only was he not fasting, he was flouting Muslim dietary laws. The omelette was enough for me; I begged
Allah to forgive my momentary lapse. At sunset, we gathered
around our family dinner tables, pretending to be weak from
hunger and thirst like the others.

The evenings of Ramadan had something magical about
them. The cafés were full. The men played a Spanish dice
game. The women paraded their children through the streets.
The city was lively. Mamed smoked cigarette after cigarette, a
brand called Favorites, the cheapest, and certainly the worst
for your lungs. On my first trip to France, I brought him a
carton of Gitanes. He gave them back, saying he hated good
tobacco. He preferred to stick to his Favorites. A few days
later, he asked me to give him the Gitanes back, explaining
that he hadn't wanted to get used to them, since he couldn't
really afford such a luxury.

Mamed and I were given more or less the same amount of
pocket money. Our parents were not rich. Mamed was always
calculating his expenses. With his taste for cigarettes, wine,

and magazines like *Hot Jazz*, he was always overspending. I
loved movies, and found a vendor in the medina who stocked
unsold copies of film magazines and newspapers. Everyone
called him "Monstruo," because of his physical handicaps.
He was twisted in every way possible, but he ran his small
shop expertly. No one dared to make fun of him, apart from
his nickname, which he had learned to accept. "So what if
I'm all twisted, I can still screw your sisters!" he would say.
He bought unsold copies by the kilo and let us rifle through
the piles. There were all sorts of French magazines, from the
highbrow *Cahiers du cinéma* and *Les Temps modernes* to the low-
brow *Salut les copains*.

The two of us swapped books and magazines. Mamed
made fun of me because I liked *Cahiers du cinéma*, which he
considered elitist. He preferred the *Ciné Revue*, and a magazine that had stories with pictures of naked women. We had
intense debates; our other friends felt excluded. They saw us
as intellectuals, interested mainly in France. They were right.
When we weren't talking about sex, we were discussing culture and politics. Despite our differences, we felt close and
complicitous. Neither of us ever made an important decision without asking the other. But oddly enough, we never
talked about our friendship. We shared most of our lives
with each other, and we were happy. It was our classmates'
jealousy that made us realize how serious our friendship was.

From time to time, Ramon would join us, commenting with amusement on our closeness. He said it was unusual, that we were closer than brothers, and he wished he could be a part of it, but the fact that he was a manual laborer made this difficult. He was wrong. It certainly did not stop us from seeing him when we wanted to pick up girls.

5

AFTER THE BACCALAUREATE, our paths were destined to diverge. With his scientific bent, Mamed wanted to study medicine. He dreamed about it. It was his calling. He got a scholarship and left for Nancy, in the east of France. I went to Canada for film studies. For the first few months, we wrote to each other a lot, then less frequently, but we spent that summer together on the beach in Tangier, just like in the good old days. We fell right back into our same routine: flirting with women on the beach, listening to music in the evening, and talking endlessly about the state of the world. We even covered the walls of the American School of Tangier with graffiti, with slogans like DOWN WITH AMERICAN IMPERIALISM, GO HOME, and VIETNAM WILL CONQUER.

That was when Mamed told me he had joined the French Communist Party. First he harangued me with hackneyed Communist rhetoric (he seemed to have lost his sense of humor again), then read Lenin to me, whom he called "the genius." He smoked just as much as before, and said how happy he was to get back to his old, unexportable Favorites. His political activism monopolized most of his time. I was bothered by the fact that he was not at all interested in my film studies. The one time he mentioned it, he launched into a diatribe: American films helped destroy the culture of the Third World, John Ford was a racist, Howard Hawks was a manipulator, and Raoul Walsh was a one-eyed visionary.

I discovered that ideological indoctrination can blind even an intelligent mind. Our discussions no longer had the same intimacy as before. The only time it came back was when Mamed talked about the girls in Nancy. He told me he was through with sodomy. The girls there were willing to have sex, real sex, and they adored Moroccans. "They say our skin glows with sunlight and desire. Can you imagine? Beautiful girls, available girls, and they aren't whores. You can talk to them like equals! Ali, you should really come to Nancy. With all my coursework and Communist Party meetings, there isn't much time for sex, but I manage. . . . The only way I betray the Party is sexually. I never screw comrades. I prefer girls who aren't communists, I don't know why. Comrades, even the pretty ones, don't turn me on. It's true, I have a better time with a laboratory assistant or a sales girl at Monoprix than with a girl from the Party. They're less hung up, too; they don't have to be begged to suck and swallow; they adore it. I have a steady girl, Martine, and two or three I sleep with from time to time. They're nice, not complicated, direct, liberated, happy. It's not like here. Remember Khadija and Zina? What neuroses! Nothing but complexes and complications! 'Don't touch my hymen!' Well, thank goodness I never did. Otherwise, now I'd be stuck with two kids. I think Khadija finally managed to get hold of an Arabic professor, you know, the guy with the bifocals, the shy one. They got married, she left school, but he makes only a thousand one hundred and fifty-two dirhams a month; I saw his paycheck. Of course, I've seen Khadija again. I fucked her, as usual, but she wouldn't kiss me or suck me. She said she saves that for her husband! They're something else, those Moroccan girls. But you know what I like about her? When you're inside her, she squeezes her thighs together and rocks back and forth. It's right out of Nafzawi's *Perfumed Garden*. I'm sure that's where she got it.

"There are also Moroccan girls in Nancy," he went on. "I prefer the nonbelievers. They're willing to do anything, and they're good in bed. In France I do everything prohibited by our religion. I eat ham, I drink Bordeaux, I have sex with married women. I forgot to tell you that my regular girl is the wife of the university accountant. We get together at the end of the afternoon, when he's still at work. It's perfect. What about you and women? With your good looks, refinement, and good breeding, you must have a lot of success. It's true, I was always a little jealous of you. Come on, I'm joking, you're not going to pout about that. You people from Fez don't have much of a sense of humor, but you're clever and calculating. Well, you know my opinion on that subject. <u>Except for you. I like you.</u>"

I told Mamed he was as racist and misogynist as ever. He pretended not to have heard me, and started talking about international politics. Then between two sentences on American imperialism, he stopped. "Miso-what? To you, women are inferior creatures. You think just like religious Muslims. I'm not religious, I'm an atheist, and I love women. Me, misogynist? That's not right, Ali. You're talking nonsense. And racist? Me a racist? Just because people with white skin get on my nerves, you call me a racist! People from Fez make everybody mad. That's not racism; that's regionalism. I'm not the only one who says that. Our Arabic teacher used to make that distinction. People from Fez are swarming all over Tangier. They have the best jobs, do well in school, and to top it all off, we're supposed to like them! No, Ali, I can forgive you for being from Fez, but don't push it."

6

I WAS STILL in love with Zina, and I had a hard time tolerating the cold weather in Quebec. This did not prevent me from having a girlfriend. A Vietnamese immigrant, whose parents had fled the war, she was sweet and exotic, spoke very little, and liked to snuggle in my arms for hours at a time. She was twenty but looked sixteen, which bothered me when we went out. Everything about her was small. She had breasts like flower buds, small, firm buttocks, and a tiny vagina. All of this was exotic to me, but our relationship was more about friendship than love. She introduced me to her parents; I was happy to have discussions with them about their lives, their exile, and their hopes for the future. They hated Communists, but they didn't want Americans in their country, either. They adored France and its culture, and were waiting for papers so they could move to some suburb of Paris.

I wrote love letters to Zina, who responded by quoting

lines from Chawki, considered by Moroccans to be "the prince of poets." Zina wanted to get married, to have children, a house, and a garden. She finally found all that with a distant cousin, much older than she, who had a job that was not exactly well-defined. Actually, like many men from the Rif Mountains, he was a kif dealer, selling potent Moroccan marijuana. Mamed wrote to me one day saying that on one of his visits to Tangier, he learned that Zina's husband had been arrested by the Spanish police and sentenced to several years in prison. From then on, Zina stopped writing to me. She was raising her child alone in a big house with a huge garden, where she had installed swings and hammocks. She spent most of her time there, reciting Sufi poetry. Mamed intimated that she never left the premises. Watched by her husband's family, she was not allowed beyond the doorstep. Her husband was kept informed of everything she did. One day he asked to see his son. One of his brothers came to pick up the boy for a visit. Zina had no say. The boss had decided. She had to obey without comment. Not even her parents were allowed to see her. They had been opposed to the marriage. "This family isn't like us," they had said, "and we're not like them. But our daughter has gone mad. She's crazy about this man."

When I heard this, I was tempted to play the hero and risk the wrath of the Rif mountain clan by rescuing Zina and her son. But where could I take them? I thought of Ramon, who had left the family plumbing business to become a real estate agent. He always had plenty of apartments to rent. Then I thought maybe Zina was happy where she was, that maybe she liked men who made her suffer. She used to tell me she liked men who were rough with her. I was never good at doing that, and some women left me because of it. Nevertheless, I let the scenario run through my head, thinking of Fritz Lang's *Hindu Tomb*, attributing to myself the strength and courage I lacked in real life.

7

DURING THE SUMMER of 1966, our youthful illusions were shattered. Mamed was arrested by the police. Just hours after his return from France, two men in civilian clothes knocked on his parents' door, asked for his passport, and took him away in an unmarked car. At that moment, I was on a plane from Montreal to Casablanca. When I arrived, there was nothing to alarm me. The police formalities and customs inspection went as usual. In Tangier, though, my parents had received a visit from a cousin who worked in the local government. He told them I should postpone my return to Morocco, but it was too late. Student activists were being arrested. Those who did nothing more than hold leftist opinions were being arrested. Mamed's parents had had no news of him for two weeks. Meanwhile, the "gray men," as my mother called them, came to our house at six in the morning to arrest me. They offered no explanations. They simply carried out their orders. We used to say that the Moroccan police had inherited all the worst characteristics of the French. They had probably been trained in France, learning how to be ruthless and uncaring.

In prison, I saw Mamed, who was almost unrecognizable. He had lost weight, and his head had been shaved. We were among a hundred or so students who had been arrested for "crimes against state security." We didn't understand what was going on. Mamed had been tortured. He had a hard time walking. The first thing he told me was that he hadn't said anything because he didn't know anything. "Usually, when you're tortured, you talk, but I didn't know what they wanted to hear. I made things up so they would stop beating me. I said anything that came into my head, but they became even more vicious. They had files on each of us dating back to high school. Someone we knew must have been a spy. With some cross-checking, I figured out who it was. Every group has a traitor. Ours was just a poor average guy getting back at a world that had not been good to him. The worst thing was that he made his career in the Moroccan bureaucracy, and ended up with an important job in the Ministry of the Interior. My conscience was clear. In any case, we hadn't done anything serious. We hadn't plotted against the government. We had just discussed the political situation amongst ourselves. They wanted information about the Algerian National Liberation Front, about our Algerian friends who had gone to fight in the war against the French. They deliberately distorted the facts to try to make us confess to serious crimes. Of course, they knew I was in the Communist Party, but the Party is legal, after all."

Mamed's look was a mixture of pride and sadness. Even after everything he had been through, he seemed strong. He hugged me tightly, and whispered in my ear, "Did you screw a lot in Quebec?" I burst out laughing. The other prisoners were not from Tangier. Some of them were common criminals who couldn't understand what we were doing there. "You didn't sell a kilo of hashish? You've never stolen anything? You never even hit one of those bastard cops?" For them, politics was an abstraction. Another prisoner, an older guy who appeared to be one of the leaders, asked: "What's politics anyway? Do you want to be ministers, and have a car with a chauffeur? You want a secretary in a short skirt, you want to smoke cigars and be on TV? When we get out, I'll get you all that. Not the title of minister, but everything else. You're decent guys. You went to school and even then they arrested you! It's crazy. This country is in trouble. I mean, things are going well, but they're making some serious mistakes. All you two did is talk. You could never kill anybody. You're too soft, too polite, too well brought up. You're no threat to anyone. I don't understand what the hell you're doing here. . . . This country is in trouble."

The guy was about fifty, and he was sure he would be released within the week. Sure enough, the guards came in one day and told him he was free. He was not a political threat; he was just a drug trafficker exporting Moroccan marijuana to Europe. When he left, he winked at us, as if to say we would see each other soon. He just had time to tell us his name, or rather his nickname, "Blondy," and that he hung out at the Café Central in the Socco, the little square that was the nerve center of the medina in Tangier.

Mamed and I spent two weeks in that prison, and then we were transferred to a disciplinary army boot camp, where we stayed for eighteen months and fourteen days without a trial. One morning, an officer came to see us and told us we had to sign a letter asking King Hassan II to pardon us. Very bravely, Mamed asked why. "We haven't done anything. We haven't committed any crimes that need to be pardoned." The officer told Mamed he was stubborn as a mule, and that he reminded him of his son, who also questioned everything. "Here you are lucky enough that our beloved king—may Allah glorify him and grant him a long life—is in a good mood, and you have the nerve to talk back? Come on, sign it. Otherwise you'll be accused of disobedience to our beloved king—may Allah glorify him and grant him a long life—and then things get serious, very serious. You're lucky I'm such a nice guy. If you'd ended up with El Lobo, the Wolf, you'd be counting how many teeth you had left."

Mamed glanced at me. I nodded my head. We signed our

names at the bottom of a piece of paper from the Ministry of Justice. One thing was certain: the king didn't even know we existed. Whether we asked for a pardon or for the hand of his daughter in marriage, the result would be the same. We didn't exist.

8

THOSE NINETEEN MONTHS of incarceration disguised as military service sealed our friendship forever. We became serious, older-seeming, more mature. Our discussions were more focused, even if we prided ourselves on a certain lightness, on our senses of humor. Now we talked about women with a sort of detachment and respect.

The food in the camp was so disgusting that I would hold my nose and swallow it fast. One day, it went down the wrong tube, and I almost choked to death. Mamed saved my life. He yelled as loud as he could for help, pounding me on the back. I turned blue and almost stopped breathing. Mamed's screams were so urgent that eventually the guards believed it was really an emergency, and they called a doctor. I was in Mamed's arms; I heard him begging me not to die. Thanks to him and his quick reflexes, I survived.

Another time, Mamed was the one who got sick. He had

terrible stomach cramps. He was doubled up in pain, vomiting a greenish liquid. We had no medicine or drinking water. He had a high fever and was shaking like a leaf. It was the middle of the night and nobody came, even though we called for help. I massaged his stomach until morning. He fell asleep while I kept massaging. The next morning, he was transported to the camp infirmary, and then to a hospital, where he stayed for more than a week. He came back pale and thin. He saw that I had been worried about him. As if to reassure me, he told me we were linked in life and death, and that nothing and no one could ever destroy our friendship.

We paid off Llrange, a decent guard, to bring us notebooks and pencils. We decided to keep a journal. Claiming he was not much of a writer, Mamed dictated his thoughts to me. It became clear that we did not have the same perception of time, or of the life we were leading within those four walls. He told me about a female ogre with plastic teeth who visited him at the same time every day, with whom he talked about his future. He made up all sorts of crazy stories. If he hadn't been sick, he might have been taken for a surrealist. But though he had a sense of form, he lacked the vocabulary.

9

AFTER WE GOT OUT OF PRISON, neither of us was ever the same. Despite our appeals to high-ranking officials, we couldn't get our passports renewed to leave the country. We were still being punished. The royal pardon had not restored all of our personal freedoms. One morning, soon after our release, we met our old friend Ramon in the hammam. He liked the Moorish baths. We told him we needed women immediately. He took care of everything, even paying for the women. Unfortunately, it seemed our sex organs were still traumatized by our incarceration. I felt bad about it. Ramon tried to reassure me, saying this often happened to him. I knew he was lying to make me feel better. The wine was OK, the girls were nice, but we were completely out of our element.

Mamed decided to go back to medical school in Rabat,

the capital. I decided to give up film studies to enroll in the
Faculty of Arts, and major in history and geography. "It's the
writing of the Earth," one of our professors said, explaining
the word "geography." He added that the Earth also writes
the story of humanity.

Student activism was widespread, but Mamed and I no
longer wanted to be involved. We were considered "veteran
conspirators," and the secret police watched our every
move. Mamed trusted no one. That didn't stop him from
spending time with a guy who was short, ugly, and dirty,
but intelligent. This guy was curious about everything,
and he went out of his way to help Mamed. I had a bad
feeling about him. He was too friendly to be honest. I
asked him about his job. He was vague and secretive. He
claimed to work for an advertising company. In fact, he
was really a cop. We found this out later when the Ministry
of the Interior appointed him head of the censorship bureau.
The whole thing made Mamed sick. He couldn't get over
it. He was mad at himself for having been taken in. "To
think he talked to me about Kant, Heidegger, film, and
art, plus he was such an ardent critic of the government
and the police!" Later, this spy made a career in intelligence. His dream was to be a writer. He wrote a few lines of
poetry, published them at his own expense, and distributed
them to government agencies. On a Moroccan television

show, he was introduced as a promising young Francophone writer.

The undercover agent had clearly been jealous of our friendship. Mamed listened to him without taking him seriously, but continued seeing him, until the guy made the mistake of criticizing me and my family.

IO

MAMED MARRIED GHITA even before he finished the course-work for his medical specialization in pulmonology. His parents were upset, and they asked me to do my best to convince him to wait. They considered me Mamed's best friend, someone he held in great esteem. Not surprisingly, I had no luck with Mamed. He was stubborn, and became resentful whenever anyone tried to make him change his mind. This rigidity annoyed me. We avoided talking about it, because when we did, he lost his sense of humor and even his ability to think straight. One day, after a discussion in which he had to admit he was wrong, he became unusually angry, saying: "Sometimes I wonder why we're friends, since we never agree about anything." I didn't take this comment seriously. He wasn't making any sense. For once I was the one to bring up his faults, something he never hesitated to do with me. We never seemed able to give each other a break. But somehow things were never even.

Mamed and Ghita's wedding took place as planned. I was the couple's closest friend. Ghita, a pretty brunette, was an unemployed sociologist. I knew Mamed wanted to have a family; he had sown his wild oats. But I was surprised that he decided so quickly. He told me it was not love at first sight. It had developed slowly—slowly but surely. He had a theory about married life that was a mixture of cliché and real reflection. For him, love blossomed through daily cohabitation. He cited his parents as an example. According to him, it was better to choose a virtuous woman rather than a great beauty who was arrogant and difficult. So Mamed settled down, and I was the only friend he continued to see on a regular basis. He had changed. He had gained weight, and he became irascible.

Little things made him angry. He no longer had any patience. Our time together was not as relaxed and easy as before. It seemed to bother him that I was still a bachelor.

I had no desire to settle down and marry a nice girl just to avoid being alone. When I met Soraya, it was love at first sight, an earthquake, a tempest in my heart, an avalanche of light and stars. Unlike Mamed, I chose beauty, which came with both arrogance and fickleness. Mamed refused to voice his opinion, claiming the issue was too personal to be discussed, even between close friends. Against the advice of my parents, I married Soraya. Her mere presence made me deliriously happy. She was intelligent and shrewd, volatile and vivacious. I had one year of peace and happiness with Soraya. She never argued with me, and she was good to my elderly parents. She was sweet and loving in public, and even became friends with Ghita, which pleased Mamed. He wanted to hire Soraya as an assistant in his clinic. I refused, thinking this might someday jeopardize our friendship. Mamed finally agreed with me, and instead hired a young nurse who wasn't particularly gracious but very efficient.

After finishing my degree, I was appointed professor of history and geography in Larache, a small coastal fishing town eighty kilometers south of Tangier. I commuted to work, as Soraya's parents had lent us an apartment in a building they owned. They refused to rent it, claiming that Moroccans were unreliable tenants. My wife worked as a nurse in the local Red Cross Society. We lived a petit-bourgeois existence, with limited horizons and limited ambitions. Once in a while, Ramon came to visit. He had married a Moroccan woman and converted to Islam. He now called himself Abderrahim, and he spoke Arabic. He said, "Ramon, Rahim—it's practically the same thing." But to us, he was still Ramon.

II

MAMED AND I had a weekly ritual: we met in a café every Sunday morning between eight and nine. First we discussed current events, then turned to gossip. From time to time, some of our old high school classmates or teachers would join us. We always avoided making political observations. We knew that police informants lurked among the cafégoers. Those were the days when Morocco lived under a sort of martial law, under which opponents of the government were arrested. Some disappeared forever. Faced with their families, the police would pretend to look for them, knowing, of course, that another branch of the police had taken care of them for good. We were haunted by this idea of disappearing forever, vanishing into thin air, reduced to a mound of earth without being officially declared dead. Lost and never found. Lost and never buried. I remember a woman who went crazy, wandering the streets with a photo of her son, refusing to go home until she found him. She slept on the sidewalk in front of the police headquarters. One day she vanished. People said the police had made her disappear, just like her son. We lived with this fear in our guts, but we never talked about it.

Mamed and I shared books and records. Some evenings we would have a drink together, either at his place or mine. Mamed liked only cheap whisky, which he drowned in soda water. These days he smoked brown-tobacco Casa-Sport cigarettes. His famous Favorites had been taken off the market, due to a documentable increase in lung cancer among those who smoked them. I got by with a little bit of Galavuiline, a pure malt whisky I bought under the table from a Jewish grocer who got it from Ceuta. When Ramon joined us, he drank Coke. Like a lot of converts, he was serious about his religion. He no longer drank rioja or ate Spanish ham. We teased him about it, and he laughed.

Mamed and I talked, argued, criticized each other, engaged in wordplay and dark humor. He was much better than I was at verbal banter, but I knew more about film and poetry. These exchanges were supposed to keep our minds active so we wouldn't fall into the lethargy most people in Tangier suffered from. Especially in those days, when everybody lived in wariness and fear. A diffuse fear, without name or shape.

Our wives saw each other, but they never became close friends. Mamed and I rarely talked about our marital problems. We avoided it because we knew instinctively that nothing good could come from such discussions. He intuited my difficulties, and I his. We remained supportive of each other, but had no need to say it or to show it publicly. There were usually no subjects that were taboo in our conversations, but we must have been thinking of Bob Marley's misogynist "No Woman, No Cry." In Morocco, as everybody knew, it was the men who made the women cry. They cried in silence. Women did not have the right to complain. In friendship, as in love, everyone needs an element of mystery. This was less true of me than of Mamed, who loved secrecy, perhaps a weakness acquired during his Communist days.

12

OUR FRIENDSHIP was about to undergo a five-year hiatus. Without any stain to its purity, it just went underground. It happened naturally, without either of us deciding anything. It was simply the result of physical separation.

Mamed was offered a job with the World Health Organization, and after some hesitation, he finally took it. He agreed with me that it would be good for him to leave the familiarity of Tangier to advance his professional life elsewhere. So he left for Stockholm on a trial basis, to see if it would suit him. As he had left Ghita behind for the time being, we made sure we saw her regularly, and frequently invited her to our home. While Mamed was away, I found a replacement for him at his doctor's office. I did the bookkeeping, paid the bills, and generally watched over his family's needs. I bought a notebook in which I kept track of all the finances to the nearest cent, informing Mamed of every transaction. He called often, and I sent him letters with every business transaction clearly detailed.

The next summer he came back, having decided to sell his office and stay in Stockholm. He sold his medical practice to my nephew, who had just finished his degree. My older brother paid Mamed's asking price without quibbling. Everything seemed to go very well. However, I began to realize that Mamed was obsessed with money, whether out of fear of having too little or mere avarice.

With my best friend gone, I felt completely alone. Our letters and telephone calls became less and less frequent. I became depressed. My wife didn't understand why I missed Mamed so much. She made occasional jealous scenes. She kept telling me to open my eyes to reality. I thought they were wide open.

One day, Mamed called from a telephone booth and asked if I was alone. I said yes. He confessed that since they had gone to Sweden, his family life had become a living hell. Ghita would become hysterical to the point of violence. I was her favorite target. She accused me of having cheated Mamed on the sale of his practice. She was sure I had exploited our friendship in order to get a good deal for my brother. Her parents had supposedly informed her of the "real price," and had even advised her to sue me for taking advantage of the situation for personal gain. I was stunned, deeply hurt. Mamed said that it was all a pretext on his wife's part to break up our friendship. I told him that my wife was jealous, too. I understood then that our relationship, built over so many years, was in jeopardy. I had fooled myself into thinking that our friendship was indestructible, that nothing could come between us.

Later, I made the mistake of repeating this conversation to my wife, who took advantage of it to pour out a torrent of emotion. You are so naïve, she told me. This guy has used you. He has always been self-interested. His friendship has never been sincere. His wife is right to accuse us. We gave her the opportunity to humiliate us. One good deed is often re-paid with a bad one. You should know that, since you've been swindled so many times by people you considered your friends, people who took advantage of your kindness. It's a weakness, when it all comes down to it. It's special form of stupidity. Now you have proof that your best friend isn't a true friend. He pretended to be on your side, but in fact al-lowed himself to be manipulated by his petty, jealous wife. You need to get rid of these so-called friends. You tell them all your secrets. I bet you even tell them about our arguments, our sex life. You can't keep a secret. You're riddled with vanity. Ah, the respected teacher, the distinguished pedagogue, the old leftie who has fallen into line with the corrupt majority! Well, thanks to Ghita, now we know. Mamed is not your friend. He is jealous and bitter, he's a slave to his wife, he does just what she tells him to, and you believe everything he says. You'd be better off taking care of your own family, saving some money so that I can go to France and see a gynecologist who can help me have a child. . . .

13

I HAD MARRIED SORAYA for her beauty and intelligence, but when she realized she could never have a child, she turned into a different woman. Our life revolved around her fertility problems. She read everything she could, wrote to specialists in France and America, tried diets to encourage ovulation, went to faith healers, and even had a telephone consultation with Jacques Testard, who had just succeeded in creating "Amandine," the first test-tube baby. She decided to try in vitro fertilization. Her parents were firmly opposed, saying this was all in the hands of Allah and we should never contradict his divine will. Her parents' opinion mattered, since they were the only ones who could afford to pay for this expensive procedure. In order to lay to rest any doubt, I underwent examinations to be sure the problem had nothing to do with my sperm. Without invoking religious principles, which I didn't have anyway, I tried to convince Soraya to adopt. I discovered that Islam forbade adoption, allowing it only in the case of a child who had been abandoned, in order to give the child a chance in life. But according to Islamic practice, the child would always remain the fruit of an adulterous relationship, and would never have the right to bear the name of the adoptive family. It had to do with laws related to heritage and incest. Still, on a practical level, corruption made anything possible. We could obtain false papers, documents, family certificates. Even if Soraya agreed to adopt a child, I told her I wouldn't do anything illegal.

The birth of Adel, Mamed and Ghita's first child, was traumatic for Soraya. She made a heroic effort to overcome her jealousy, yet it took nothing but the slightest remark or reminder to set her off—a pregnant cousin, a neighbor's inquiry, a television ad for diapers. She would become depressed all over again.

I don't know whether my friendship with Mamed suffered from this. Distance and infrequent contact had preserved our bond. When Mamed called to ask how I was doing, he talked as if we had seen each other the day before. I avoided telling him about Soraya's fertility problems, just as he avoided discussing his marriage. Mostly, we talked about cultural events. He recommended books and films he was able to see before they came to Tangier. I caught him up on the local gossip. He liked to know what was happening while he was gone. It was as though Tangier belonged to him.

A city of seduction, Tangier lashes you to its eucalyptus trees with the old ropes left by sailors at the port; it pursues you as if to persecute you; it obsesses you like an unrequited love. We talked and talked about Tangier. We knew that without our city, our lives would be meaningless. We needed to know what was going on there, even though we knew that nothing really earthshattering ever happened. Tangier was like an ambiguous encounter, a clandestine affair hiding other affairs, a confession that doesn't reveal the full truth. It was like a family that poisoned your existence as soon as you got away from it. You knew you needed it, without being able to say why. Tangier, the city that had given birth to my friendship with Mamed, harbored an instinct for betrayal.

I told Mamed the latest gossip, and I was amused because I knew how much he missed it all. Brik had married Ismael's widow. Fatima had been abandoned by her husband after an affair with a young French official. The Regnault high school had been repainted. The Cervantes Theater was still run down. Allen Ginsberg had passed through town to see his friend Paul Bowles, and they were seen smoking marijuana at the Café Hafa. The French-language newspaper, the *Journal de Tangier,* had changed hands. The Lux Cinema was closed for repairs. The Mabrouk had been demolished in order to build a new nondescript building in its place. Tangier had not had a governor for six months, and nobody noticed. King Hassan had promised to visit Tangier, but no one believed him.

Hastily constructed new buildings had gone up, though they were uninhabited, and no one knew who owned them. The American Consulate had closed. Riots had broken out in the working-class area of Beni Makada. Barbara Hutton's house had been sold. Yves Vidal had given a big party in his palace in the casbah, while his friend Adolfo had celebrated the construction of a swimming pool on the roof of his house with yet another memorable dinner. Tennessee Williams drank so much one night that he fell asleep on a doorstep of the Rue Siaghine. I caught a glimpse of Jean Genet at the Café de Paris. Francis Bacon bought every kind of alcohol he could find at the Epicerie Fine market. A turf war among drug dealers had left three dead at the port. Momy was getting thinner and thinner, driving around town in a pink Cadillac with an overly made-up blonde in the back seat. I saw Hamri in a café, and he assured me that his paintings would be worth a fortune after his death. Ramon was still in love with his Moroccan wife, and had become a true Muslim, to the chagrin of his Spanish family.

The Hotel Minzah had been sold to an Iraqi. There was supposedly an Interpol warrant out on him. The Café de Paris had new furniture; the Porte Tea House was still closed. A new radio station had started up. The Rif Hotel was barely staying in business. The Colonnes bookstore was still in the same place. So was the Claridge, though the café was not as good as it used to be. The wind from the east had been particularly strong this summer. Gibair no longer flew from Tangier to Gibraltar. There were only four Indians left in the whole city; two of them had a shop in the Socco Chico, in the medina, and the other two sold watches on the Boulevard Pasteur in the new part of town. The Siaghine church had closed its doors. The synagogue nearby was still open, but had only a few visitors . . .

Tangier has lots of new neighborhoods, buildings constructed with no planning, no trees, gardens, or parks. If you saw that, Mamed, you would be upset. King Hassan came through town without stopping; his train dropped him off at the port, where he took the boat to Libya. People waited for him all day long, in the heat, burned in every sense. Elizabeth Taylor celebrated her birthday in Malcolm Forbes's palace in the casbah. And me? What about me? Well, I'm still teaching. I got a small promotion, five hundred dirhams more a month, sent to a new school. Now I'm at a teacher's training school in Tangier.

14

I NEVER CELEBRATED MY BIRTHDAY, but Mamed always sent me a card and a present, usually a record or a book. We were born the same year; he was three months older. When he moved to Sweden, the tradition ended, which seemed perfectly normal to me. It was part of the change in the tone of our friendship. It had become both more essential and less a part of everyday life, on standby, waiting to prove it had not lost its intensity.

One day, Mamed called asking me to check on his sick mother as soon as possible. He wanted me to see if her condition really warranted a trip back from Sweden. He told me that his brother often exaggerated the state of his mother's health, to make him feel guilty—the sort of thing that happens in families. Would I go and see her, talk to her doctor, and report back to him? He had more confidence in me than in his brother; I was more objective. He said he would call at the same time the next day. He added that he had spoken with his father, who was much less dramatic about it all, but perhaps because his father worried any time Mamed got on an airplane.

In fact, his mother's condition was extremely worrisome. Her diabetes was out of control. She barely ate anymore, but her blood sugar was high. She had all kinds of complications, she no longer recognized anyone, and the doctors couldn't do anything more for her. I told Mamed to come home immediately. He arrived two days later. At that point, his mother was a little better, and he looked at me as though I had misrepresented her condition to get him to come back to Tangier. Mamed was his mother's favorite, and she was waiting for him to come home so she could die in peace. She told him so, and then died in his arms. Mamed hugged me and cried, asking me to forgive his doubts about my judgment.

Ghita, seven months pregnant, had remained in Stockholm. I took care of the funeral arrangements as if they had been for my own mother. Mamed was profoundly affected, crying and expressing guilt about having been absent for so long, something his brother did not hesitate to point out. He stayed with us during that week in Tangier. Something about him had changed, though I was not sure what. He still smoked as much as before, and he drank a lot. He had found some cheap cigarettes in Sweden, had become thinner, and spoke passionately about the Scandinavian welfare state. It was a real democracy, he said, without corruption, without lies from the government, no beggars in the streets, very few alcoholics. The Scandinavian sense of civil rights was the stuff of dreams for an Arab or Mexican, he told me, and immigrants were given the opportunity to learn Swedish, to have decent housing, and to be a citizen like anyone else. What shocked him, he said, was that despite all this, the Swedish still complained about their system. They talked about the corruption in industry, for example, or complained that social security did not take care of everything. They would point out that old people were not treated well in the hospitals, citing the story of an elderly couple so unhappy with their medical care that they wrote a letter of complaint, then got in a boat and drowned themselves off the coast of Gothenburg. "Imagine if all the sick people in Morocco did that. There would be no one left!"

And yet he missed Morocco. "I miss the smells, the morning scents, the sounds, the nameless faces we see every day, the warmth of the sky and the people. I'm really torn. My working conditions are ideal. I'm well paid, even though more than half my salary goes to taxes. My child is being raised in a country with real justice, where he has the right to disagree with the government, to speak freely, to believe in God or not as he chooses. He is free, but is he happy? Maybe I'm transmitting my doubts to him. Ghita is very happy. She's made friends; there are lots of radical women who do charity work—she volunteers for an organization that helps exiles.

I'm the one who's dying of boredom. I miss Tangier. I hate to admit to this ridiculous nostalgia. You know what I miss the most? Our discussions in the Café de Paris and the Café Hafa. I'm not the only one. Whenever I meet other Moroccans in Sweden, the only thing they talk about is Morocco. They think nothing has changed. It's nostalgia. They find spices in the Iranian and Turkish markets and make *tagines.*"

"Moroccans in Sweden are never satisfied," he continued. "They forget that Sweden has given them a chance to remake their lives. But I'm sure if they came back to Morocco, they wouldn't last more than twenty-four hours. They are completely screwed up. I don't want to be like them, so I'm going to come home at least twice a year. I have to find a balance between that country, with its ideal democracy and this one, with its widespread corruption. There has to be a balance between Sweden's justice and this country's sleazy compromises, between Scandinavian solitude and invasive Mediterranean communality. It's a question of bridging the gap. The trick is not to lose your cultural identity while you take advantage of real democracy. Remember, the Swedes lost their prime minister, Olof Palme, precisely because he was so accessible to ordinary people. He was gunned down walking out of a movie theater. How different is that from Morocco? Here even an obscure deputy minister would never be seen in public without his bodyguards. Traffic stops; sirens blare. These people despise ordinary citizens."

15

BEFORE HE LEFT TANGIER, Mamed went to see my parents. He examined my father, who was having trouble breathing, and prescribed some medicine, wondering out loud whether it would be available in Moroccan pharmacies. If not, he offered to send it from Sweden. My mother gave him a box of little cakes she had just made, insisting: "They're good, especially in the winter. Take them with you. I hope you like almond. And look, take these two rolls, fresh from the oven. Homemade bread is good. I'm sure your mother used to pack food for you. I've always done that for my children. It's important to eat well. Come back and see us. If you need anything, remember you have a home here, too. Come here, my son, so I can embrace you and give you my blessing." Mamed's eyes filled with tears. He hugged my mother and promised to return.

We received a package from Mamed with the medicine for

my father, a pretty cashmere shawl for my mother, and a pen for me. Soon after, Mamed's second child was born. He called him Yanis, telling me over the phone that it was like Anis, Arabic for companion, but it was also the Greek name for John. "He's a little Swede who will make his life here. It's different for me. I'm too old to start over, so I go through the daily motions, do my job well. I no longer try to bridge the cultural gap between Sweden and Morocco. I'm tired. I'm still thinking about whether or not to have Yanis circumcised. It's supposed to be better in terms of hygiene. Now don't get any ideas from those old Fez families who kidnap little boys and have them circumcised without their parents' knowledge. I'm only telling you this because I know you could do it. By the way, say hello to Ramon for me."

I finally convinced Soraya to adopt a child. We went through the usual procedures, legal and illegal. It took six months, and then, one day, my Rif Mountain friend Azulito (his nickname came from his blue eyes) brought me a birth certificate and another legal document confirming the adoption of our son, Nabil. We had to lie, telling everyone that Soraya had had a difficult pregnancy, and that she'd been confined to bed rest for the last six months. We didn't tell anyone he was adopted. That was the price we had to pay for Soraya to reclaim her zest for life, her inner peace, her easy disposition. I told Mamed the truth. He sent Soraya a magnificent bouquet of flowers.

The next summer, Mamed came to see us with gifts for Nabil. He had changed a great deal physically and coughed all the time, claiming it was air pollution. He had good cough drops, he said, but he had left them at home.

Once again, we fell right back into our old summer routine—meeting at the Café de Paris in the morning and Café Hafa in the afternoon. We talked and joked about everything. But one evening, while we watched the sun set on the Spanish coast, he suddenly became serious. "I think I've made a mistake," he said. "I never should have left Morocco for Sweden. I'm lost. I've seen how you can live differently, and in many ways better than here, but it's not my culture, not my traditions. My wife and children have adapted better than I have. I'm depressed there, unhappy here, dissatisfied everywhere. The whole thing has been a failure. I'm not well. My children don't speak a word of Arabic, even though they're supposed to have learned it at school. They think of Morocco as a vacation place.

I don't want to grow old in Sweden. I think I'm going to come back. They need lung specialists here. What I would really like to do is retire early and come home. I doubt my wife and children will join me, but we all have our own paths to follow." He punctuated his words with a nervous, dry cough. I had given up talking to him about his health. He was certainly well qualified to know what was going on inside his lungs.

16

SORAYA SEEMED HAPPY, and she no longer got angry over little things. Nabil was growing up in a peaceful household. I had no complaints about my wife, but I still felt the need to have a secret affair with Lola, an Andalusian woman who worked at the Spanish consulate. I didn't feel I was betraying Soraya, and had no guilt whatsoever. Lola looked as if she'd stepped out of a Modigliani painting. She lived in her own world. She said she did not belong to anyone, and that she preferred romance to friendship. In fact, her sensuality attracted many lovers. I first met her with Tarik, a physical therapist, probably the only openly gay Moroccan in Tangier.

Well aware of her charms, Lola was always the one to make the first move. In the beginning, I tried to resist. I liked her, but I had long since given up on sexual relationships that weren't going anywhere. Yet I felt a strong desire to respond. Why mire myself forever in the pseudo-comfort of a routine life? After a while, I realized that I had gone along out of a desire to imitate Mamed, not to upset him. I had decided to remain faithful to my wife and not give in to carnal desire. Yet I was bored with the routine of it all, the nights Soraya and I would have sex, the nights she had headaches, the nights I went out with my male friends. I couldn't stand this routine any more. The temptation of risk and adventure became too great. I didn't say anything to Mamed about this when I gave him the latest news from Tangier. When he asked about me, I told him everything was fine, Soraya was fine, there was nothing to report.

A sort of mutual modesty had emerged between Mamed and me. We no longer joked about our private lives. Sex became something we never talked about. I was tempted to tell him about my affair with Lola, but I knew he might be shocked, so I said nothing. It was impossible to know which of the two of us had the upper hand in our relationship. We complemented each another; we needed each other. We both acknowledged this, and we took a certain pride in it. Like me, Mamed preferred friendship, a bond we chose, to the family bonds imposed on us. I had no reason to complain about my older brother, but we were not friends.

Lola liked to make love everywhere but in the bedroom. She had spots all over the city, as well as on the Old Mountain, where she liked to have sex. The first time, we did it in her car. I hated it. It reminded me of the frustrating sessions with Zina in my youth. Lola had thought of everything: condoms in the glove compartment, cloths dipped in eau de cologne, towels, even a club hidden under the seat in case we were attacked. She was an expert. I left her car stiff and disheveled, feeling like I had just ridden the bumper cars at a carnival.

The second time, she took me to an abandoned hut near Donabo Park. She pulled a blanket and all the other necessary accoutrements out of her car. She was highly aroused. When she came, she cried out in Arabic, "Hamdoullah," and in Spanish, "Gracias a Dios," thanks to God. This made me laugh. I had barely caught my breath when she turned over on her stomach and told me to take her from behind. That evening, my knees hurt.

Another time, Lola arranged to meet me in the office of the Spanish consul, who had gone back to Madrid on family business. She was naked under a transparent *jellaba.* "Fuck me here, on the boss's desk, on top of his files and old newspapers. Don't touch anything, or move anything," she said. "Here. I want you. Shut the door, but don't close the curtains. The light is beautiful."

With Lola I traveled through time and space. She gave me enormous pleasure. I had forgotten how much I enjoyed making love. As in our youth, I thought of Mamed, who must have experienced the same feelings. Once we had shared a girl. It was a game. Afterward, we asked which one of us she preferred. She laughed and said it was like making love with the same man, which we took as proof of our virility. The sharing stopped when we both married. The time for games and swapping was over. We entered a serious phase—that is, a boring routine. It was to escape this routine that I had my affair with Lola.

Every night, I came home exhausted. I went to bed thinking how much energy I needed to satisfy this insatiable woman. I joined a gym, less to exercise than to have an alibi in case Soraya started to get suspicious. I began to enjoy the intrigue of my double life. No one knew about it. I called Lola at her office every other day at 5 P.M., let the telephone ring three times, hung up, then called her back. "Will you fuck me tonight?" Lola would ask. "I'd like to do it in a Turkish bath, so try to reserve one just for the two of us. Unless you'd like me to ask Carmen to join us . . ."

She knew how to excite me, to unsettle me, to push me toward dangerous new paths. Now I was obsessed with the idea of doing it in a Turkish bath. I didn't know Carmen, but apparently she was a divorcée who had not had sex for a year and was ready to do anything to end her long stretch of abstinence. Physically, she was very different from Lola, with big breasts and a small ass.

Carmen met me instead of Lola. She took my hand and led me back to her place. After Lola's less conventional tastes, I rediscovered the comfort of a large bed. She asked me a favor. "Let me smell you. It's been so long since I've smelled a man. Don't mind me; this is what I've missed." She stuck her nose in my armpits, breathing deeply, then rubbed her nose along the rest of my body, lingering a long time between my thighs. I let her do it. I was excited. She writhed in my arms like a wounded animal, holding me tightly. "I don't want to take Lola's place," she said, "but we're very good friends, and she gave me this as a present. This is the first time I've done anything like this. I was a faithful wife, but when my husband left me for our young housekeeper, I became depressed, and I didn't want to touch a man. I touch myself every evening, but nothing can replace a man's skin, his smell, his sweat, his breath, his caress, even if it's clumsy. You've made my friend-ship with Lola even stronger. I don't know whether two men would have done that out of friendship. I doubt it. Men are much more selfish, less courageous, and they never share any-thing. Thank you and good-bye. I have no intention of seeing you again. This was a just a deal I had with my friend. I'm going to find another man and live normally again."

17

THESE CLANDESTINE AFFAIRS restored the vigor and sexual ap-
petite I had almost lost. I asked myself whether Mamed
would have appreciated what Lola had done. He might have
when we were younger, when we reveled in fantasy, when our
illusions were still intact, and when our imaginations offered
flights of escape.

Our friendship had become too serious. Mamed, who in
the past had been such a joker, a master of wordplay, always
ready to make us laugh, had definitely changed. After his
mother died, he came back to Tangier often. He came alone
and stayed with us, and he drank too much. He had become
extremely sensitive, got angry easily, and continued to smoke
cheap, disgusting cigarettes.

One evening, when Soraya was already asleep, Mamed
started to cry. He blamed himself for having left Morocco,
for having been away during his mother's illness. He started

to confuse everything, drunk from all the whisky. Perhaps he was also suffering from depression. The next morning, he had no recollection of what had happened. He told me I had made the whole thing up to make him feel guilty, to destroy his mood. I said nothing.

During his stay, he learned that an apartment on the fifth floor of our building was for sale. He went to see it, and decided to buy it then and there. He called his wife, who was less than enthusiastic about owning a place in Tangier, but she ended up agreeing. The apartment belonged to Soraya's parents. They sold it to Mamed for below market price. They knew he was my best friend. Mamed went back to Sweden, asking me to take care of the interior decoration and the furniture. Soraya and I worked to get the apartment ready, sending Mamed photos of rooms as they were finished, along with fabric swatches for the sofas and the curtains.

The apartment would be finished by summer. I put up the money for the remodeling, which involved borrowing from my bank. Mamed did not know about this. I waited until several days after his arrival in Tangier to show him the bills. He coughed more and more these days, and his face had taken on a strange cast. His wife told me that Mamed had refused to stop smoking and drinking, despite the advice of a colleague, a professor of medicine who worked in the same hospital. When I presented Mamed with the bills for the work on the apartment, he pushed them away, indicating that this was not the right time.

Our two families spent the summer together, sharing every meal. One evening, I arrived late; dinner was waiting. Mamed shot me a reproachful look. Even my wife never looked at me in such a cold, suspicious way. After dinner, he suggested we take a short walk on the Avenue d'Espagne. There was something dark about him. Something had changed in the way he spoke and thought. "I've studied the bills you gave me. I even showed them to Ramon. What you've done is wrong. It's unworthy of our relationship. For a long time I've felt that something like this might happen. I wasn't sure you were capable of abusing my trust this way. Don't interrupt me. Let me say what's on my mind."

He paused, as if he were about to give up the idea of saying anything, and then he blurted out: "You took advantage of my being gone to cheat me. You did it as though I were some kind of idiot, probably telling yourself, 'He's far away, he's in Sweden. He's not even Moroccan anymore. He won't suspect anything. He'll swallow everything.' But I'm more Moroccan than you are. I'm suspicious of everything and everyone. Actually, in Sweden I learned that money is money, and there's no shame or hypocrisy in talking about it. It's not like our charming country: 'No, no, let me pay. I insist! Look, we're not going to be like Germans who split their restaurant bills.' No, in this country we're generous, hospitable. We'll even go into debt to avoid seeming poor. We sell our animals so we won't lose face in the village when it's time for a religious feast. Well, I'm not who you think I am. I've finally understood. Your friendship is worthless. You've always looked out for yourself. I've tried to tell you that friendship is not a series of profitable little calculations. But you and your wife and your in-laws had the nerve to sell me the apartment at thirty percent above the going rate, pretending to give me a good deal because we were friends. And you were an accomplice. You forgot to mention the commission you made on the deal."

Mamed stopped talking, then continued hammering away. "Don't interrupt me. Don't say anything. I know what you'll say, that in the name of Allah and the prophets you're an honest man, that you even lost money on the whole deal, that I should thank you for taking care of everything. Well, I let you do it as long as I thought you were my friend, not a traitor or a thief. No, let me finish. You can talk later. Wait until I've said my piece. Everything between us has been ruined. First it was your wife, bothering us with her jealous scenes. You were always complaining about them. You would even call me at the hospital when you knew I was making my rounds. You would leave a message. 'Please call your friend in Tangier.' And I did! I called you back. What an idiot!"

Mamed was out of breath, his eyes red. "It was only later

that I realized how cheap you are, that nothing came out of your pocket without careful calculation. That brought me back to our childhood, our youth. When we first met, I protected you. I liked you because you seemed fragile. You never had any money on you. After school, you hung around so you could have an afternoon snack at my parents'. You claimed you liked the bread from the Spanish bakery better than your mother's, but you were really trying to save money. I knew you had a problem, but I told myself that one day you'd get over it, you'd be a decent guy, generous, unselfish. But you stayed the same, cheap and opportunistic. When it came to political commitment, you lied, too, skipping political meetings on the pretext that your mother was ill. You were never very brave. You always arranged things to appear to be someone you're not. People always knew they couldn't count on you! And now these bills!"

There was a brief pause in Mamed's monologue. "Those bills are all fake. Are you going to tell me that the carpet came from Ceuta, and the fabric for the sofas came from Gibraltar? Did you go there? No, you sent Ramon, the newly-converted good Samaritan. He did this little job for you, for me. I should thank him. But Ramon wasn't in Ceuta, and certainly not in Gibraltar. I've checked the prices, and they've all been upped by twenty to thirty percent. Yes, my dear friend, the one I used to play with, in whom I confided my romantic adventures, it turns out that all this childhood friend wanted was to make a couple of thousand dirhams behind my back. You thought, 'He's an easy target. He's a doctor, he has better things to do than check these bills.' But don't kid yourself. I listened to my wife, and we conducted a little investigation. What you've done is shameful. I guess you decided to reimburse yourself for the computer you bought me for my fortieth birthday. You said, 'Learn how to use a computer. It's amazing'. At the time, I thought it was an expensive present, but you had it all calculated in advance to cheat me.

"I was blind, refusing to listen to my intuition, or my wife's. I believed everything you said. To think we served time in prison together for our ideals, for the values we shared. You should never have gone to prison for your ideals, since they are totally insincere, a lot of hot air, a lot of talk, not serious at all. You're a phony. Don't try to defend yourself. To think I always wanted the best for you, that I put your interests above my own, above those of my wife and children. You were the friend, untouchable in my eyes, whom I preferred to my own brother. I was proud of you, especially when you rejected the easy life of bars, friends, prostitutes, and more bars. I thought you had settled down, that you never cheated on your wife. That's what I thought. Now I know not only that you betrayed my trust, but that you lead a double, maybe even a triple life here. Sure, you told me a little about that Spanish woman, but the others? Anyway, now I know about them, too. Rumors? Don't interrupt me. Here in Tangier, everyone knows everything. Nothing is secret. You can try to hide things, to take precautions, but in the end everyone finds out. You might say that your sexual transgressions are not my business; that's between you and your wife. But they're low and common. They've opened my eyes to all the rest of it.

"And the rest is huge. It stinks. The little tricks in order to spend the least money possible, to be two-faced. With you, there's always another way out, so you can work the situation to your advantage. But it's not really possible, my friend. You are careful with your health: you don't smoke, and you barely drink. Even sex is carefully calculated according to what you think your body can handle. Everything is measured. You don't get sick, so you don't have to pay a doctor. It works for you—you're in good health, which is not my case. I cough when I get out of bed, when I talk, when I go to bed, and even when I sleep. I drink a glass of whisky every night. I am killing myself slowly, methodically. But I'm happier than you are. No, leave me alone. Don't try to help me. It's fitting that I would be coughing during our moment of truth. I've emptied my lungs to tell you how much you disgust me, how much I regret these thirty years of illusions. Don't forget anything I said. Get away from me. Don't try to help me. My family and I are going to sleep somewhere else. This is a final good-bye. I never want to hear your voice again. I never want to hear anything more about you or your family. This is it, forever."

18

WHEN I RECEIVE a severe emotional shock, my body reacts physically. My saliva dries up. I feel something bitter in my esophagus, and then I start hyperventilating. I have to sit down and drink some water. Mamed left me, coughing so violently he was staggering. I walked into La Valencuela, the ice cream parlor of our childhood, and asked for a bottle of water. The owner, who knew me, sat down beside me and asked if he should call a doctor.

"No," I replied, "Dial 36125, my house, and let me speak to my wife." I must have drunk a whole liter of water. I was still sweating, but my mouth was no longer dry. I felt a knot in the pit of my stomach, and I worried that it would come up and choke me. I was pale, my vision was blurred, and I shook as if I had a fever. Soraya arrived, and threw herself into my arms, in tears. "What happened to you? Did somebody mug you? There's no blood, you're not wounded, but you're as pale as a ghost. What happened? Talk to me. Call an ambulance!"

I stopped her from calling anyone. There was no point. It was just an emotional shock. It was not serious, just a house in ruins that had collapsed on me. I was full of dust, the roof had caved in on me, there were fallen beams. It didn't feel bad at the time. I didn't realize what was happening to me. Everything was collapsing around me. First some stones, then a whole wall, then parts of doors, after which I was buried in the rubble. It was like an avalanche of snow, like a fall into the void, surrounded by chunks of hard ice, and yet I couldn't find the ground. I heard words, but I couldn't call for help. I had the impression that some strong hand kept me from opening my mouth. So I continued my freefall into the void, while I sweated and my mouth became dry.

When Soraya and I got back to our apartment building, there was no trace of Mamed and his family. They had gathered their possessions and left. I noticed that there were traces of blood in some spit in the bathroom sink. The house smelled of medicine. My wife held me in her arms and cried. I did not want to speak, to discuss what had happened. In fact, I could no longer speak. I had lost my voice. I had only one desire, to record on paper what Mamed had said in those last hours, to write everything down, without worrying about order or logic. I spent the night writing. Soraya understood that I should not be disturbed. When morning came, I closed my notebook and slept until the afternoon. I must have lost at least a kilo. The sweating continued even during my sleep. I took a shower, put the notebook in the safe, and watched an old Hitchcock film about somebody falsely accused of a crime, played by Henry Fonda. Truth hung by a thread between light and darkness. Daily life seems simple, whereas in reality it is quite complex. All it takes is for appearances to become intertwined with emotions, and you become the center of an invisible, hidden vortex swirling you into a nightmare.

I knew the Hitchcock film by heart, and I let myself be swept away by the story, in which anyone, however common or anonymous, could become the victim of a bureaucratic error, a terrible injustice. It was my story.

The next morning, I got my voice back. I went to the café for breakfast as usual. I saw Ramon, who was worried by my state of mind. He asked so many questions that I ended up telling him what had happened. He was an upright man, warm and sensitive. He listened without saying a word. I saw the shock on his face. He could not understand what had happened. Neither could I.

19

A FEW DAYS LATER, I felt the need to write to Mamed. I drafted several letters. I wanted to avoid sounding pathetic or spiteful. Above all, I knew it would be a mistake to try to respond in a legalistic, point-by-point way. He knew his accusations were false, but why did he feel the need to make them? What lay behind this sudden drama? What was he really trying to say? I wrote the following:

Dear Mamed,

Tell me about the real state of your health. Your cough sounds bad to me. But as a lung specialist, you know this better than I do.

You and your family left, vanishing from the apartment like shadows. I am not angry with you. I would just like to know what happened, and why you picked this particular evening to try to destroy me. I refuse to defend myself and to prove to you what you know better than anyone else. I was hurt more by your state of mind and body than by what you said. We know one another well enough not to make up stories, or to stage inquisitions in public. Our friendship has a strong foundation. Your accusations are unworthy of our long history together.

I will let you rest. When you feel better, call me, or tell me when I can call you. We need to be able to speak calmly so that everything is clear and unambiguous.

I embrace you as always.

Your faithful friend

Mamed's response took less than a week to arrive. A curt, brief letter arrived in a recycled envelope:

If you consider yourself my friend, you should know that I am not yours.

I want nothing further to do with you or your family.

I have examined the bills and done the accounts. You owe me a total of 34,825.53 dirhams. This is the difference between what you really paid for the renovation and decoration of the apartment, and what you made me pay. Deposit this sum tomorrow at the Ouladna Orphanage.

Do not call me again. Do not write to me again. I have put the apartment in Tangier up for sale. There you will find the computer and printer you gave me to try to buy my friendship. They remain in good condition. I barely used them.

Farewell.

II

Mamed

I

I WILL ALWAYS REMEMBER the first time I met Ali. He was wearing a tight white shirt and blue polyester pants, and he spent recess reading a book, not talking to anyone. "You should play, have fun. You can read at home tonight," I told him. "I don't like to play, I never have fun, and I'd much rather read a good book," he replied.

It wasn't clear to me what the future would hold, but I had the feeling that this boy with the white skin and carefully combed hair would become my friend. I told him that he could follow me into the bathroom to smoke, but he refused, and gave me a little lecture: "My mother's brother just died from lung cancer, because he smoked a pack a day—American cigarettes. They smelled good, but they were fatal." I laughed. He smiled. I patted him on the back. He put his hand on my shoulder, and took a few drags of my Favorite. He choked, and swore he would never smoke again.

The following Friday, Ali invited me for couscous at his parents'. He lived in a small house at the top of one of the cliffs overlooking the ocean. I suggested he also invite Sam, who could get us into the Whiskey à Go Go nightclub, even though we weren't old enough and didn't have any money to spend there.

Sam was not a great student; he was smart, but lazy. He had a phenomenal memory. Once he read a page of the phone book and recited it without a single mistake. But when the teacher asked him to recite a Baudelaire poem, he garbled all the lines and gave up, telling the teacher it was too beautiful for someone like him. He came from a very poor family, and he worked nights at the club, which didn't give him much time for homework. He proposed a deal to Ali: "You write my essays, and I'll get you into the nightclub whenever you want. I'll even introduce you to pretty girls who aren't virgins."

Female virginity was our obsession. Girls willing to have sex were rare, and we knew about them only because they already had a steady boyfriend or were in their last year of school. They came to school wearing makeup and perfume. We watched them from a distance, making lewd comments. At the same time, we knew they were untouchable; they were French, and older than we were. One of them was named Germaine, and we called her "over the hill," as she had been dumped by her boyfriend and after that had sex with other boys. She had red eyes, perhaps from crying, but I was sure it was because she had sex all the time.

Ali pretended not to be interested in girls. I knew he was shy, and that he practiced what we called in Arabic "the secret habit." One day, at my house, I suggested a masturbation competition. The idea was to think about one of the beautiful high school girls, say her name, and go at it. Sam shouted "Josephine," our high school queen. I called out "Wanda," thinking of her flashing brown eyes. Ali remained silent, but he looked as if he was concentrating. "And you?" we asked him. "Who's your favorite?" He answered softly, "Ava Gardner." We were stupefied. Ali was aiming high. But after all, why not, it was an imaginary game. We turned our backs to each other, right hands grasping our penises. The idea was to ejaculate at the same time. Sam yelled insults to his imaginary sex object. I moaned. Ali screamed, "Yes, Ava, yes!"

This game was depressing, though, and we left deflated. We wanted relationships with real girls. Sam offered the services of the prostitutes at the nightclub where he worked. "How much?" Ali was as poor as I was. "Free," Sam replied, "It's a little favor they'll do for me. But it has to be in the middle of the day, when the club is closed." We chose the day and the time. When we got there, three women were waiting for us, not old, not young, not ugly, not beautiful, probably naked under their gray *jellabas.* They were waiting for us the way they might have waited for the bus. It was clear that they had no interest in having sex with fifteen-year-olds, but they were willing to do it for Sam. Ali walked out, saying he would wait for us outside. Sam pulled out his penis. I closed my eyes, and threw myself at the other two, feeling them up underneath their *jellabas.* I didn't have time to do anything else, I ejaculated so quickly. Afterward, I didn't feel well. Sam had entrusted his penis to the other woman's mouth. I went outside to join Ali, who was reading a book by Anatole France.

2

ALAIN WAS THE TALLEST boy in our class. He had broad shoulders, blue eyes, a studied gait, and a lock of blond hair that he played with to seduce girls. He wanted to become a movie actor, but the war in Algeria ended his youthful dreams. He came from a good Catholic family who liked Arabs, as long as they kept their distance.

Alain was my first real fight. He was discussing colonization with Ali, spouting all sorts of idiotic comments. He said that France was a great power bringing civilization to Algeria, a country of illiterate peasants. "Algeria is France. Our country will never leave Algeria in the hands of peasants who only know how to slit throats. My older brother is proud to be fighting there for freedom, and when he comes home, I'll go myself. If you don't like it, what the hell are you doing in a French high school? Why didn't you stay in your Koran school? *Bougnoule!*"

I didn't know this word, but I knew it was an insult. Ali, shy and slight as he was, attacked Alain with a few tentative punches. Alain pushed him to the ground with one blow. Ali bled from his nose. I motioned to the racist French boy that it was time for a real fight. The students gathered in a circle while Ali was taken to the infirmary. Alain was much stronger than I was; I had blood everywhere. Sam pulled us apart. He could see I was going to be massacred.

All three of us were suspended for three days. The principal used the incident as an excuse to lecture the entire student body about events in Algeria. He sounded reasonable, presenting the issue objectively. Some students inferred that he seemed to be against Algeria remaining French. Two months later, he was called back to France. We never saw him again. Alain didn't wait to be drafted. He had already enlisted, and was serving in the Aures Mountains, where the fighting was particularly grim.

We were in twelfth grade. Before Alain left, he made up with Ali and me. We kissed each other on the cheek. While we were waiting for the results of our baccalaureate examination results, the son of the French consul told us that Alain was dead. We were distressed. Ali and I wanted to do something, go see his family, take flowers to his girlfriend, but we ended up doing nothing. Someone quoted Paul Nizan: "We were twenty years old, and no one can tell me this is the best time of your life." We heard Sam say with a little laugh that he was not interested in politics. At that moment, I decided it was time to get involved.

3

MY UNCLE HAMZA was very French, in an old school kind of way. He spoke the language of Descartes perfectly, quoted the classics, and was an impeccable dresser. At the same time, he had an excellent knowledge of classical Arabic. He said he was a nationalist. I didn't know he was also a Communist. He explained that there were many positive aspects of Marxist doctrine, some of which could be applied in Morocco, to help the country out of its underdevelopment, to fight against the worst social inequities and the corruption of the government. He was convincing, opening my eyes to a new way of thinking. I talked to Ali about these ideas, who met them with more reserve.

I spent my first year at school in political meetings and demonstrations. This worried my father, who decided I should continue my medical studies in France. He had an animated discussion with my uncle, whom he accused of dis-

tracting me from my studies, of being an atheist, and of es-
pousing ideas imported from Moscow. Hamza responded
calmly, but my father remained angry. Having used up his arguments, my father insulted Hamza by calling him a *zoufri*,
because he was still a bachelor. Hamza seized the opportunity to explain the origin of this word. "Zoufri" comes from
"worker." It was too bad that the petit bourgeoisie associated
this with debauchery and vice, he said.

Ali was hoping for a scholarship to study in Canada. He
was in charge of the Rabat film club, and sometimes I helped
him. Ali made the posters advertising the films, and I put
them up. I enjoyed his film-club meetings. He spoke intelli-
gently and eloquently about films, their political role, and
their importance in twentieth-century history. I admired
him, and discovered a different person, not shy at all, confident and at ease before an audience. He had a particular passion for films directed by Satyajit Ray, an Indian he
considered an artist with an international appeal. Ali
thought that Ray's films also expressed Moroccan concerns
and our desire for justice. Once he even went as far as to say
that Ray was a Moroccan filmmaker, with unusual talent. In-
troducing *Pather Panchali*, Ali quoted a phrase he had read
about the film in a magazine: "They can pressure poor people, but they can't take away their talent." Ali argued that the
exoticism of this Indian universe was a mirror distorted by
geography but one that invited us to see our own exoticism:

that is, our problems. Well-informed about all aspects of film, Ali never forgot the social and political reality of our country. He made the link between life and art, between the real and the imaginary.

During our political meetings, Ali was meticulous and precise. His one flaw was impatience. He could not tolerate people who came late, or people who could not think on their feet. I was proud to be his friend, though his image of me as the well-bred son from a good family got on my nerves. The fact that he came from Fez accentuated his feeling of being different, a sort of disguised arrogance. I did not know Fez, and I had no interest in going there. The people of Fez considered themselves the sole heirs of the Andalucian Golden Age of Muslim civilization.

We knew a cop had infiltrated our group. He was a student, someone we knew, who ate with us in the university cafeteria, who joined our political debates. He was both intelligent and mean. We were wary of him, but he played the game better than we did. He was short, very thin, ugly, and wore bifocals. He had no luck with girls, but he drove expensive cars and often invited girls to private soirées. Claiming to be the son of a wealthy industrialist, he said he detested his father, who exploited his workers, underpaid them, and did not allow them to unionize. He was the one who reported on our activities to King Hassan's political police. This was 1966, one year after the student riots of 1965, when thousands of high school and university students demonstrated against bad education legislation. They were joined by the unemployed and other dissatisfied citizens. General Oufkir, the interior minister, suppressed the rebellion with machine-gun fire from a helicopter. Hundreds were killed. Afterward, there were thousands of arrests.

One morning in July 1966, the day after my return from France, two men in civilian clothes arrested me at my parents' house. My mother cried. My father controlled himself, trying to negotiate with the police. There was nothing they could do, they said. Orders were orders, and these came from high up. "We have to arrest him to interrogate him, and then he will be sent off to do his military service." My father choked. "What military service? This is Morocco." The reply was instantaneous. "Well, your son will be starting a new tradition. Think of it as an honor for the family."

We all knew the names and faces of people who had been arrested and were never heard from again. My mother threw a roll out the window into my hands.

I spent fifteen days at the mercy of the police. They beat me. I thought about my parents, about Ali and Hamza. I knew the authorities had opted for total repression. General Oufkir was in charge. We had committed no crime. We just had some ideas for helping our country emerge from poverty and paralysis.

4

THERE WAS NOTHING to indicate that the military base where
the jeep let me off was a disciplinary boot camp. I got there
at the end of the day and waited in an empty room. Around
two o'clock in the morning, an enormous man appeared. His
head was shaved. "I'm Commander Tadla, and I'm in charge
here. I report to no one, not even the camp commander."

He left me with a corporal who told me to take off all of
my civilian clothes and put them in the sack he threw at me.
"You'll find everything you need here to become a soldier," he
said to me. Another soldier arrived with a little case. He was
the camp barber. He proceeded to shear me like a sheep, then
shaved my head, without saying a word. By three o'clock in
the morning, I had become someone else.

Early the next morning, Commander Tadla called all of us
together and gave us an unforgettable lecture. "You are just
ninety-four spoiled kids. You're being punished. You wanted

to be smart-asses, and I'm going to teach you a thing or two. There's no daddy and mommy here. You can yell all you like; nobody will hear you. In this place, I will dress you and change you. You'll no longer be spoiled kids, queers, children of the rich. Here Commander Tadla rules. Forget all that liberty-democracy crap. Here the slogan is: 'We belong to Allah, our king, and our country.' Repeat after me . . ."

I looked around for Ali, but I couldn't find him. I was sure he'd be in the group punished by General Oufkir. Afterward I found out he had been in the infirmary, where they were changing his bandages. The barber who shaved him had used a rusty blade, and Ali had several deep gashes on his head.

When I saw him, I scarcely recognized him. He had lost weight and his head was bandaged. He embraced me. We were in the same barrack-room, but not in the same section.

In our group there were students, teachers, a lawyer beginning his career, an engineer who had refused to kiss King Hassan's hand at the end-of-the-year university reception. "Punishment" was the euphemism for what they were doing to us. We were quarantined, and at the mercy of lower-rank officers, some of whom had served with the French army in Indochina. Most of them could neither read nor write, and they spoke a mix of French and Arabic. The ones who had been in Indochina were nicknamed "the Chinese." They never spoke to us, but they beat us occasionally.

Once I was clubbed on the head for trying to protect Ali.

I was worried about his health. A young doctor, sent by the French government, forced Commander Tadla to send Ali to the military hospital in Rabat. Tadla had some respect for the French officers who were employed by the Moroccan army for their technical skills.

Ali left the camp with a military escort, as if he were some kind of dangerous criminal. Tadla warned him: "Not a word about the camp. Otherwise. . . ." He didn't need to finish his sentence. We knew what he was capable of. He had spies everywhere, and he was often called to Rabat to report to his commander. We presumed he was in direct communication with General Oufkir. They had known each other in Indochina. It was rumored that Oufkir admired Tadla's force in repressing the Rif Mountain riots in 1958. Tadla was said to have killed people with a saber. In the camp, his stature was maintained by his acolytes. Even the camp commander was afraid of him. He didn't show it, but the day Tadla left the camp, the commander called us together and told us we should never defy Tadla.

5

I FELT VERY ALONE during Ali's absence. He was lucky to be in the hospital. The rest of us led a Sisyphean existence. Our job was to transport rocks from one end of the camp to the other, to build a wall that other detainees would immediately demolish. As soon as we'd finish, we'd start all over again. The corporal who filled our sacks with rocks was sadistic. He chose the heaviest rocks, and if we paused for a second, he kicked us in the ass. Camp rules forbade us from helping anyone who collapsed under the weight of the load. It was hot. We were thirsty. We were not allowed to speak to one another. The distance from one end of the camp to the other was two kilometers.

Ali came back in relatively good shape, looking almost normal, ready to rejoin the ranks of the "punished." He told me about his stay in the Rabat hospital, where he had met the son of a colonel. As soon as he had learned that Ali came from El Hajeb, he asked to switch rooms. Ali had returned with a book that a doctor had given him, *Les Liaisons dangereuses*, by Choderlos de Laclos. The doctor said that if he needed a mental escape from the camp, there was nothing better than this twisted love story. It would let Ali travel through time and space.

Once a month, we were given a pack of cheap Troupe cigarettes and a good meal. Since Ali hated tobacco, he reluctantly gave me his pack. Smoking was the only pleasure the camp allowed at certain times. Ali preferred to think of a woman he said he was in love with. He confided in me. Not knowing when we would be released from the camp, we made no plans for the future. Ali liked talking about this woman whom I didn't know. What with her absence and the sufferings we were enduring, this woman took on legendary proportions. Ali compared her to his idol, Ava Gardner. Sometimes he hallucinated. I did nothing to bring him back to reality. Like all of us, he needed to dream, to escape from reality when he could.

I was not in love, and I had not left a girlfriend behind. As time passed, I imagined a magnificent creature named Nina. Ali suspected she did not really exist. He listened to me, and suggested we arrange for the two women to meet, so they could talk about us. He said we would have to wait for a full moon, and that we would conjure them by thinking about them with all our might. Unfortunately, on that night we were being punished collectively; one of the detainees had tried to scale the wall to see a prostitute. Tadla ordered us into the courtyard, and we had to stand at attention until sunrise. Half the detainees fell over from the strain. Ali and I managed to stay the course, precisely because we were able to escape mentally. Despite our best efforts, we did not succeed in staging a meeting between the two women. We needed an isolated place, where we could summon tremendous concentration. As the night was ending, I thought I saw the two women walking hand in hand through the ranks of detainees. They gave water to some men, brought others back to their feet. They were perfumed and scantily dressed. They vanished as soon as Tadla showed up.

6

SIX MONTHS AFTER OUR ARRIVAL, General Oufkir decided to send us to the officers' school in Ahermemou, a mountain village north of Taza on the way to Oujda, near the Algerian frontier. Tadla said nothing about our destination in his good-bye speech. "You guys are no longer a bunch of weak women; you're men—strong and patriotic. Now you understand we will not tolerate Communism in our country. You're going somewhere else, I don't know where, in the secret army. You'll be with men who will continue to work on you the way I have, so no messing around—don't screw up. We bury troublemakers in holes with only their heads left above ground. They can breathe, but they fry in the sun, and they're only good for the hospital. The Chinese taught us this method. Very clever, the Chinese."

We had seen soldiers buried with only their heads above the sand, left in the heat of the day. Tadla had made a point of showing them to us. We already knew how cruel he was. We didn't need further proof.

The officers' school of Ahermemou was quite different from El Hajeb, the camp we had left. We sensed that the worst of the torture was over, and that our reeducation would now take place under more humane conditions. We slept six to a room. I asked the officer in charge if I could be in the same room as Ali. No problem, he said. We arrived on New Year's Day. It was snowing. The commander gathered us together and spoke to us in good French. He had been educated at the military academy in St. Cyr, in France. He was refined and hard, without being vulgar. This officer knew why we were there, and what he was supposed to do.

"I know who you are. I've studied each of your dossiers. I know that your political activity is incompatible with the monarchy and the prerogatives of the king. Here, there are no politics. I was chosen to complete your reeducation, and I'll tolerate no discussion or rebellion. I'm in charge here. I don't know any of you, and I'll follow orders without compunction. The slightest infraction by a single individual will lead to collective punishment. Here, you wash every day, you're on time, and you obey orders. A word to the wise should suffice. Fall out!"

The commander was a more sophisticated version of Tadla. Young officers took charge of our instruction. We were given pens and notebooks. We underwent military training, deprived of any civil liberties. We could write to our families, but our letters went through a censorship office. Ali wrote to his "fiancée," who did not respond. The day he suggested I write to Nina, I realized he was beginning to lose his mind. I wasted no time bringing him back to reality. He knew that he sometimes became delirious, and admitted that he had no more sensation in his penis. Same for me. We tried to calm ourselves by putting bromide into our disgusting morning "coffee," made partly from chickpea paste. I told him that this kind of punishment regimen was designed to make us regret, for the rest of our lives, whatever we had been arrested for. It had been refined by penal experts, so that we would end up eating sand, losing all confidence in ourselves. The idea was to brainwash us by the time we left, so that we'd be ready to obey, without ever doubting or contesting anything again. This was the method used by Mao and Stalin. We were perfect victims. So what difference did it make whether we had erections or not? Where could we go with our excited cocks? I'd forgotten what a woman's body looked like, I'd forgotten what sexual desire and pleasure felt like. We didn't know when—or if—we would get out of there. It was torture, psychological torture. But Ali had to hang on, just as I did. Otherwise, we would be giving them the satisfaction of seeing us beaten down, defeated.

There was one Jew among us. He had probably been arrested in error. The police and the army did not like to admit their mistakes. He was there, said nothing, spoke good Arabic, but found himself alone. His name was Marcel. Ali and I tried to talk to him, but he preferred to remain apart from the group. On the first day of Ramadan, the month of Muslim fasting, he finally spoke up, asking to talk to the officer in charge. He had no reason to fast during the day, like the Muslims. His case was heard in Rabat, where it was decided that he'd be allowed to eat during the day. When the officer in charge told him he had won this privilege, Marcel thanked him, but said he had decided not to exercise it. "I'm like the others," he said. "Even if I'm not Muslim, I will observe Ramadan." For him, it was a matter of principle. After this, he felt more at ease, better integrated into the group. But the commander did not appreciate this show of solidarity. He ordered Marcel to eat a piece of stale bread in front of the rest of us. Sure, Marcel was a Moroccan, the commander barked out, but not a Muslim. "You're a Jew, so act like one!"

Marcel lowered his eyes, and bit into the hard, stale bread. After the second mouthful, he vomited. The commander put him in solitary confinement for three days.

7

OUR SENSE OF SMELL got used to the nauseating odor of camel fat, but I couldn't stomach food cooked in it. Ali ate only bread and noodles. We were all fragile, but Ali took it to the extreme. Of course, there was no question of protesting or expressing ourselves. We fantasized about simple meals on a terrace in the summer, with beautiful girls, eager bodies, and light hearts.

After all the inmates suffered digestive problems, the commander assembled us and told us he was changing the cooking fat. "Camel fat is good for nomads, but you're sedentary types, so I've given orders that from now on the food will be cooked with beef fat. It's more practical; if you get diarrhea, I can't use you. Consider yourselves lucky to be able to eat as much as you like. Others would give a lot to be in your place. I know, you're not really made for this job, but I don't give a damn. You were rebels, so now you're paying the price. At ease! Be prepared. Tomorrow our military maneuvers begin. I'm telling you, we expect three percent 'wastage'—lost lives. Don't be part of this three percent. A word to the wise should suffice." The commander loved this expression.

Ali and I remained inseparable; sometimes Marcel would join us. The head of our section allowed us to gather in groups. We weren't plotting anything; we just needed to be together, eat together, throw up together, share our anguish and our hopes, and think about our eventual release.

Ali received a letter from his father, brought to him by a lieutenant, the son of a distant cousin, passing through Tangier on his way to a mission at Ahermemou. Ali cried when he read it. He showed it to me:

My dear Ali,

Since you left, your mother has gotten sick. She no longer sleeps, she's obsessed with your absence, and she imagines the worst. The doctor has discovered respiratory problems and high blood pressure.

I had to go to Rabat several times to find out what had happened to you. It took me six months to learn where you were, and why you were being held. None of the military officials seem to know anything about your case. It's a special matter under the personal control of a general, they told me.

I have also seen the parents of your friend Mohammed, whom you call Mamed. They are worried, too. We are all living in agony, and the worst is that we know nothing. We hear you are allowed to write one letter a month, but we have received nothing.

Your father embraces you, gives you his blessing, and prays to Allah and the Prophet to help you out of this tunnel. Allah is great and merciful.

8

A FEW DAYS LATER, I came down with a strange fever. I felt hot, I shook, I sweated, and I became delirious. Ali spent nights at my bedside, wiping my forehead with a wet tissue. At the infirmary, they accused me of dissembling, in order to avoid the military maneuvers. So I left with the other soldiers, but after an hour on the march, I collapsed. Ali helped me up, and he managed to convince the lieutenant to send me back to the infirmary. Without Ali's help, I probably would have ended up in the ground.

It was December, and freezing cold. Because the commander had found an insulting comment about him on one of the walls, he called us all together, told us to strip down to our underwear, and left us outside for an hour. Then he came back and screamed: "Whoever wrote that insulting crap, step forward. If you don't, you'll all stay here until you freeze to death!" I saw Marcel walk toward the commander, who stopped him. "No, it's not you. It's written in Arabic. I know you speak it, but you can't write it. Get back in line. No need for you to help a Muslim."

An hour later, we were falling like flies. Ali was already on the ground. The commander came back. "Not bad. Courageous. You show solidarity. No traitors, no tattlers. You're dangerous. Now I can see why you're here. Well, I'll figure out another way to deal with this." We returned to our dormitories, mocking his threats. In the end, he did nothing. Perhaps the writing on the wall told the truth: "Commander Zamel, the queer commander." Rumor had it that he was one of the captain's lovers, or vice versa.

Rumors. Nothing but rumors. We heard some of us would be released on January 3. There would be a list, determined by General Oufkir and maybe King Hassan himself. Unfounded rumors, but they kept our captive minds occupied. Marcel, the Jew, would be let out first, as there was no reason for him to have been there in the first place. The engineer who had refused to kiss the king's hand had apparently been pardoned by the king. So had the lawyer. Where did these rumors come from? It was the commander who started them. It was also rumored that the lieutenant who brought the letter to Ali had made an alarming report to the authorities on the commander's abuses.

On January 3, no one was released. On January 8, Marcel

was summoned by a doctor who had come from Rabat. The next day he was escorted back to his home.

Our turn came on January 15. We were summoned for a medical inspection. The commander called us into his office and offered us coffee. It was nothing like the black, bitter liquid they served us in the mornings; it was real coffee. I inhaled its aroma several times before I drank it. He looked at us as if we were Indians setting foot in white civilization for the first time. "By now you are men, citizens who have seen and understood how things work in this country. I have to confess that as officers, we were not happy that the army was serving as a punishment force. The army is not a reeducation center, or a prison in disguise. The army is a family with values, of which the most important is dignity. We were ordered to destroy your dignity as citizens and opponents of the regime. I want you to understand this. I know who you are. I have respect for your convictions and even for your plight. This country needs justice. I'm sure we'll meet again one day, not for an exercise in repression, but to work together for the good of our people, who deserve to live in dignity and prosperity. We Moroccans have become used to living bowed down. It's time we stood up straight. Do you understand?"

We were speechless. Was this man testing us, trying to find out what we would do when we left this place? He certainly wasn't required to make this kind of speech. He got up and we stuck out our hands to say good-bye. He opened his arms and embraced us. We left his office stifling a laugh. Had the guy gone crazy, or what? Or was he simply arranging a date with destiny?

In fact, that was it. Three and a half years later, on July 10, 1971, he led a group of officers in an assassination attempt on King Hassan at Skhirate, where the sovereign was celebrating his birthday. Ali and I were at the beach with friends that day. When we heard the radio announcer proclaiming the end of the monarchy, we were scared. We knew only too well what those military officers who attacked the king's garden party were capable of. Morocco narrowly escaped a Fascist regime.

After our release, it took us a day to get back to Tangier. Our two families got together and organized a celebration in our honor. Ali and I couldn't fathom what was happening to us. A few days later, our Spanish friend Ramon organized another party. Our hearts weren't in it. Our minds were still back at the camp. It was impossible to erase the scars of that long and cruel period in a few days. Ramon felt bad. Our detention had lasted eighteen months and fourteen days. Ali and I were bound together for life. After that, our friendship was held up as a model. We needed to learn how to forget the trials of that period, to regain a taste for life. Spending time with Ramon would help distract us, clear our minds of this nightmare.

9

AS LONG AS YOU have not been tried and acquitted, you remain a suspect. My father wanted to understand what had happened. He wanted to do something, alert the international press, sue the army. He was angry, and my mother pleaded with him to calm down. "What?" he shouted. "My son has been arrested, tortured by the police, and sent to a disciplinary boot camp. We had no news from him, then one fine day he is let out as if nothing ever happened; he is followed by the police, our house is watched, our telephone is bugged, and you think we should accept these arbitrary practices of the state?"

He did not stop. "I demand that they restore my son's honor, his innocence. He didn't kill anyone. I demand that his passport be returned so he can continue his studies in France. Things should be clear. Is he innocent or not? What is this 'royal pardon'? Either he was guilty of committing a crime for which he must answer, or he did nothing, in which case the judicial system should say so, and acquit him."

My father was right, but in Morocco things aren't logical. I returned to my medical studies in Rabat. Ali abandoned the idea of film school. He decided to pursue a degree in history and geography at the College of Arts. Our different schedules meant we did not have much free time together in Tangier. We saw each other during vacations. Ramon came with us on our nightly outings. He made us laugh with all his jokes. He could have been a comedian.

It was at Ali's house that I met Ghita, the woman who would become my wife. She was the daughter of a cousin of theirs by marriage who had come to spend a few days' vacation in Tangier. Her beauty intrigued me. She was silent, and rather observant. She had a way of looking at people and things that sometimes embarrassed me, as if she were mentally undressing them.

Ali told me to be careful. Yet how could I not immediately fall in love with this woman? I stole glances at her, and told myself I would risk damnation for her, I would do anything . . . it was as if a veil had been placed over my eyes. I had become as good as blind.

I needed my friend's opinion. I needed his blessing, his approval. I could deal with my parents, but it was important that Ali approve of my marriage. I knew that many friendships were destroyed by marriage. Wives were sometimes jealous of their husband's friends. I wanted to avoid this at all costs.

I lit one of my bad cigarettes, a nervous tic, and asked Ali what he thought. He advised me to wait a little longer before committing myself, to go out with her, flirt, but not to be in such a hurry. "I find her very beautiful," he said. "That's precisely what worries me. A beautiful woman is often more preoccupied with her beauty than with her home. The most important thing is to see whether she really loves you as much as you love her. If things start out one-sided, it's hard to achieve a balance. Marriage is not about passion. It's about daily compromise. Of course, you know all that. We've talked about it endlessly. It's understandable that you're in love with Ghita. She is beautiful, intelligent, discreet—everything your previous conquests weren't. But marriage is serious. It's forever. No more affairs on the side, no more infidelity."

Ghita and I sometimes went out with Ali, and she would bring her sister. We would go to the tea room at the Minzah Hotel, where we would eat pastries and laugh. I held her hand. The following summer, I married her. I hadn't finished the training for my medical specialization, but as a wedding present, I was given a passport. The city's governor brought it to me himself. Without thanking him, I asked, "What about my friend Ali?" It was Sunday, he replied. "Tell Ali to come and see me on Monday at six P.M. sharp."

We left for our honeymoon in Spain. Ali flew to Paris for an internship with the French Federation of Film Clubs in Marly-le-Roi.

10

BEFORE I OPENED my own medical office, I worked for the public health system. There I discovered another Morocco, one of misery, shame, and despair. Consultation was free, but we had no medicine. People who could afford it went to private clinics. Those who were even richer went to France. The rest died.

The first year of my marriage brought happiness and pleasure. When Ghita became pregnant, I had a hard time telling Ali. He had married Soraya, a pretty girl who seemed calm and poised, but was apparently unable to have a child. Ali believed in telling the truth. A pregnancy isn't something you can hide, he said. If Soraya has problems, it's not Ghita's fault. Not only did he tell Soraya the news, but he held a little party for Ghita and me at his home.

Ali suggested adopting a child. Soraya didn't like the idea. She was only twenty-eight, she said. They should wait, try again, and then, if necessary, consult specialists in France. I told Ali that adoption was difficult in Morocco, but like everything else, there were ways to make it happen. A few months later, my wife put Soraya in touch with an orphanage. The two women went to speak to someone there.

They came back in tears. Soraya was shaken. They had seen babies of all ages, smiling, ready to go home with anyone willing to pick them up and hold them. Later, I learned that Ali and Soraya had adopted Nabil, a six-week-old boy.

Ali helped me a great deal when it came to setting up my practice. I was uncomfortable about this. He made too much of it, which got on my nerves, but I tried not to let it show, thanking him, saying, "You really shouldn't have." He told me not to use these petit-bourgeois clichés. His in-laws offered to sell us an apartment. Ali and I had less time to talk than before, but our friendship still seemed to have the same strength. We had become inseparable, but sometimes I needed to be alone. Ali couldn't understand this. I couldn't ask him to leave me alone. I often had the impression that I had become his second family.

Between Ali and me, money had never been a problem. Neither of us was rich, but we had plenty of money to live comfortably, nothing to complain about. My practice was doing well. I had borrowed some money from the bank to buy equipment. We led calm lives, no disturbances, no dissention between us. We had one rule, which was never to talk about our marital problems. We knew that couples meant conflict more than anything else, and that married life could slowly strangle the love that had spawned it. I tried hard to make my marriage a success, to compromise, and that surprised Ali. We did not need to discuss it; I could read his thoughts easily on his face. Ali had a face like an open book, which sometimes worried me. His face betrayed his strong emotions. Ali was the type who couldn't hide what was bothering him, what was hurting him. As soon as I saw him, I knew what he was about to say. Occasionally I would be wrong, but never about serious things. He had the ability to share my life, my world, and my imagination to an extent that fascinated and worried me at the same time. This superior form of intelligence was impressive. I envied it. But over time, his intuitiveness bothered me. We were two open books. We could see right through each other, and deep down I didn't want that.

Ali taught at a teachers' training college while he continued to run the city's film club. He had become friends with two elderly women who owned the Librairie des Colonnes, the bookshop on the Boulevard Pasteur. They had a passion for film and literature. Ali loved to spend time with them, which he often told me about. The three of them had tea once a week, to discuss what they had been reading and their mutual passion for the films of Bergman, Fritz Lang, or Mizoguchi. This was still in the days of movie houses and the big screen, before video ruined films by putting them on televisions.

The day I was offered a job with the World Health Organization in Stockholm, I asked Ali where I could find Bergman films. Movies sometimes reveal more than any other guide to an unknown culture. Ali managed to arrange for me to see several films on Sunday mornings at the Roxy Theater. After the sixth one, I felt truly enlightened. I was going to live in another world, strange and exciting, a society consumed by metaphysical anguish, but highly evolved. Ali gave me these film lessons with a delight and excitement that did not conceal his pride in teaching me something I did not know. I was annoyed, but I never showed it.

II

ARRIVING IN SWEDEN from Morocco, the first thing you notice is the silence. It's a silent culture, without disruption or disorder. I looked for people with dark hair, and saw only blonds. The men and the women were much taller than Moroccans. Their silence, the whiteness of their skin, their clear eyes and distant look, their gestures, their routine politeness, and their respect for rules . . . I discovered a culture of individuals. How marvelous! In this society, everything had its place, and one person was as important as another. I fell under the spell, even though I suspected that beneath the surface there had to be problems. But I saw this country through my Moroccan eyes, the eyes of a doctor who had suffered a great deal from the lack of respect for the individual, and from the lack of rigor in a society built on a thousand little compromises. Here in Sweden, there were no secret deals.

You worked hard and respected the law. You did not try to undermine it and bargain with it.

My medical colleagues greeted me with enthusiasm. Not with the slaps on the back, the embraces and rote courtesies of Morocco. Their enthusiasm was sincere. I was not the only foreigner. There were Africans, Indians, Asians, and various Europeans. While we studied, we learned Swedish but spoke to each other in English.

My wife and son joined me six months later. Ali and Soraya had taken care of them in the meantime. I had been obliged to leave them for a while in Tangier, but this caused me some concern. I felt that I was becoming indebted to my friend, never a good thing in a friendship.

After a year in that cold country, I missed Morocco. It's crazy, but the things I missed most were things that had previously bothered me: the noise of the cars, the shouting of the street merchants, the technicians who messed around trying to fix elevators without admitting they knew nothing about them, the cheese, the old peasant ladies who sold vegetables from their own gardens. I missed Ramon and his jokes, especially when he stuttered. I even missed the cops at the intersections, whom you could bribe once in a while. I missed the dust. Strange how Sweden had no dust, or smells coming from the restaurant and household kitchens. Swedes eat smoked or marinated fish, salads, dried meat, cold vegetables. I missed the density of people in the fish market in the

Socco Chico at Tangier, with its stench, its poor and struggling clientele. I even missed the beggars and the handicapped on the streets.

When I was a child, my father always held up Sweden as the perfect example of liberty, democracy, and culture. There I was, walking in the snow, hoping to find a friend to talk to. I thought of Ali, and wondered what he might be doing at that moment. He might be watching a good movie, or reading a good book, or maybe he was bored; maybe he was envying me. I went into a telephone booth and called him.

I needed to hear his voice. It was important. I was overcome with doubt. I was full of melancholy. He was sleeping. Scarcely a minute passed before he understood my state of mind. He told me that he had had to take a sleeping pill and put cotton in his ears to block out the awful Egyptian soap opera his neighbors were watching. They refused to turn it down. After shopping at the market, Ali had had to walk up five stories with his load of groceries. The elevator was not working, because the landlord refused to pay the maintenance charges. The upstairs neighbor had bribed the building inspector to allow him to build a studio for his son, even though it was dangerous and illegal. There was no cleaning service in the building, because the doorman had divorced his wife and married a young peasant woman who refused to work.

"I'm only talking about the daily annoyances," Ali said. "I

haven't even mentioned the state of the university. There's a new phenomenon: the rise of the old, bearded advocates of totalitarian Islam. You see? You don't know how lucky you are. No one has any respect for civil rights here. I have to put up with this fucking soap opera. I have to accept this mediocrity, because there's no other choice. Don't even think of coming back. Work, live, travel, enjoy your freedom, and forget Morocco. If you do come, come in the summer as a tourist. Visit the plains, the mountains. We don't even have a decent museum. We have sunshine, but I'm sick of sun. I have to go now."

I told him to give Ramon a hug. "Tell him to write down his latest jokes and send them to me. I'll write to you tomorrow. May Allah keep you safe, you and your family."

I felt reassured, and I realized I couldn't indulge in nostalgia. Once again, Ali had come to my rescue. He wrote me a long letter right away, full of local gossip. He ended with an unhappy tirade about married life. I understood he had another woman. After we had both gotten married, we rarely talked about women or love. A kind of modesty had come between us. Those discussions belonged to our youth; we had settled down.

It took me a while to understand that Ghita did not appreciate our friendship. In a certain sense, this was normal. Jealousy has a wide scope. I had often been jealous of Ali, because he was more cultured than I was, because he came from a partly aristocratic family, because he was better-looking than I was, and because his marriage had made him rich. I was jealous of his inner peace, or what passed for it. In fact, I knew Ali too well, and that bothered me. When I couldn't sleep, I would ask myself: Why should I be jealous of him? He's not famous, he's not a professor of medicine, not a great writer. Why do I feel this way? I'm annoyed at him, and I don't even know why. It's bizarre. I'm jealous for no reason. But how did this happen? Insomnia is cruel; you can't think clearly. Jealousy can arise from the simple fact that the other person exists; never mind who he is or what he does. All of this made me bitter and unhappy. I felt like a boat listing in the heavy seas. I was drowning under the weight of dangerous feelings, but I did nothing to push them away.

12

WHEN YANIS WAS BORN, Ghita suggested that we return to Tangier for the baptism. When I spoke to Ali, he thought it was an excellent idea, and was ready to take care of everything. "Don't do anything," he said. "Just tell me when you arrive, and that's when the party will start. We Moroccans are good at this. We know how to celebrate, entertain people, make a feast. Everything is an excuse to slaughter chickens and sheep, to cook enough food for a whole tribe. It's our trademark. I bet when a child is born in Sweden, the family has a glass of wine with friends, and that's it. At least, from what you've told me, Swedes don't seem to care a lot about food. They'd rather drink. Yanis, that's a nice name. I hope the Moroccan consulate agrees to it, when you go for his birth certificate. We have Anis, companion, but to me, Yanis is the name of the great Greek poet Yanis Ritsos."

Ali never missed the chance to show off his literary background—or rather, to point up my lack of one.

When I told Ghita what Ali had said, she took it badly. "What now?" she said, "Why is *he* planning the celebration for my son? My parents are there. They won't understand why an outsider is getting involved in our family affair. That's it. Call your friend and tell him to back off."

Ghita's reaction was out of place, her anger excessive, her language stronger than her thoughts, but actually she was right. I gave in and called Ali, who was not at all surprised. It was normal, he said. Soraya had staged the same scene with him. "It's as if the two of them were in cahoots. Forget it. Your in-laws will do it."

In the end, the party was a sad event. I could feel the tension among the guests. I smoked two packs of cigarettes a day. In Sweden, I had cut way down, but here my nerves were frayed.

In the afternoon, the two of us sat on the terrace of the Café Hafa. Old memories came back to us, as if we were watching a film. We relived the images, the sounds, the smells of the past. The evening mist obscured the Spanish coast in the distance. I coughed quite a bit, even though I had my cough drops. I was tired, but couldn't tell if it was physical fatigue or moral torpor. I observed Ali, and read the same lassitude on his face. For the first time, I wanted him to go away. I didn't feel well. I couldn't stand myself, and I couldn't stand him. I wanted something intangible. Perhaps I wanted the sort of serenity Ali always seemed to have.

It was during this trip that I decided to buy an apartment on the fourth floor of Ali's building. I knew it belonged to Soraya's parents. I took my wife to see it, and she liked it. The apartment had a good view of the port and the ocean beyond. In front of Ghita, I asked Ali to deal with everything: to negotiate the price, and to supervise the renovations. He hesitated for a moment. "I won't do anything without Ghita's permission," he said. "Of course she'll want to be in charge of decorating her own house. I won't do anything without running it past her. We'll see about the price before you leave."

Once we bought the apartment, I authorized Ali to proceed with all the necessary work. Our arrangement was clear. Soon he was bombarding me with faxes of estimates and bills, sending fabric swatches in the mail. You would have thought it was his own apartment. His enthusiasm annoyed me.

That winter, the first symptoms of my illness appeared. They couldn't hide the truth from me. I understood the prognosis, and I knew better than most what was going on in my lungs. Dr. Lovgren, who had become a friend, told me that he believed in telling his patients the truth. "You've seen the X-rays. We're lucky to have caught it early. You should start chemotheraphy this week. You're young. But then, lung cancer seems to favor the young. Talk to your wife about it. We won't tell anyone here. You'll have the best treatment available. Don't panic. I can see the shock in your eyes. That's always the way it is. It's good to be well-informed; but when we doctors hear this kind of news, we're as stunned as any patient. I think we can beat it. I have a good feeling about this. I know that's not very scientific, but even among scientists, intuition and the irrational are important. You can continue to work as usual; just slow down a little. Whatever you do, don't give in. Be positive, fight back. You know a positive outlook can make a difference. You know all this, but I'm telling you as a friend."

13

I REMEMBERED the story of the avalanche that surprises you, then engulfs you. I remembered what my mother told me: beams fell on my back, and I was stuck in the ruins. I felt crushed, powerless in the face of the facts, the fatal blow. I should have prepared myself better for the inevitable. Lately, I smoked without pleasure, but I clung to the habit. My lungs needed the nicotine, the tar, the deposits of poison eating away at my bronchial tubes and suffocating me. I had been warned, but I always thought I would escape this fate.

I looked around, focusing on random objects. They were there, solid and eternal. I went out to the square near our house, and watched the passersby walking with a certain, determined step. Where were they going? How did they feel? There had to be at least one person my age dealing with the same anguish! I saw only people in obvious good health. Their bodies bore no pain. Even the old woman who had so much trouble walking was not sick. I was sure I was the only sick person in the entire city of Stockholm. Illness imposes an intense feeling of solitude. Ultimately, we are alone.

I needed to talk, to confide in someone. Above all, I knew I couldn't tell Ali. He would drop everything and come to take care of me. I would read the progression of the illness in his eyes. His face would become a mirror; I couldn't bear the thought. We knew each other too well to risk this. Ali was not a good actor, and he was incapable of lying or hiding his feelings. No, I couldn't tell him. My wife was already depressed. I would tell her after I began treatments. I walked into a bar. It was noon, time for the open-faced sandwiches and salads they eat in Sweden.

A man was sitting alone at the bar with a large glass of beer. I singled him out because he was around my age. He had to be between forty and forty-five. I spoke to him in the casual, superficial way people do in Sweden. He raised his glass. I ordered a glass of white wine. He was an engineer from Gothenburg whose work had brought him to Stockholm. He was exactly my age: forty-five. He was in good health. I told him I had just learned I had lung cancer. He raised his glass again, and patted me on the shoulder. He said nothing, but his eyes were full of sympathy.

I left the bar staggering, walking like an old man. I felt an intense desire to be near my mother, to go to her grave and talk to her. I had tears in my eyes. I coughed and it hurt. I was tired, troubled, with no desire for anything. I thought of all the food I liked, which I denied myself, for fear of getting fat: vanilla pastries, Moroccan cookies, glazed chestnuts, whole-wheat bread covered with butter, fresh goat's cheese, grilled almonds, Arab dates filled with almonds, Turkish figs, fig jam, lemon tarts, foie gras, preserved duck—all fatal to the liver. . . .

I felt nauseated. Nothing interested me anymore. I needed time to prepare myself for this blow and to find a way of dealing with it, this cruel assault that had been coming for a long time. Curiously, what I wanted was a cigarette, but I didn't have one on me. I thought about stopping someone on the street. No, that was it for cigarettes.

14

WITHOUT TAKING SLEEPING PILLS or tranquilizers, I slept soundly, not even getting up to urinate. I must have been either overwhelmed or relieved. I did not dream. My wife was surprised. She said I must be tired, that I must be getting sick, a bad flu or something, and I should consult our friend Dr. Lovgren. I could have chosen that moment to tell her the bad news, but I didn't dare. She was happy that morning; she was going off to her yoga class, and I didn't want to upset her.

I went to my office in the hospital, where we were evaluating a disastrous situation in Bangladesh. A strange parasite was attacking people's lungs. I was among those designated to investigate. I was eager to go, thinking it would distract me from my own problems, but Dr. Lovgren decided otherwise. His pretext was that he needed me in Sweden to help him analyze the data the other doctors in the team would be sending back. I realized then that my case was hopeless. When the two of us were alone, I asked him point-blank: "How long do I have?" He said he wouldn't know anything until the end of the first chemotherapy treatment.

At the hospital where I was being treated, I met another Moroccan, as sick as I was. His name was Barnouss. He had removed the final "i" from his name to appear more Nordic, but with his mop of black hair and dark complexion, it would have been obvious to anyone that he was Maghrebin. He was less worried than I was, and talked to me as if we were old friends. "Here, my compatriot, I have confidence. It's important to have confidence in a country and its health system. That way, you're halfway to being cured. In Morocco, I have no confidence in the medical system. I'm sick even before I get sick. I mean, even the thought of finding myself in the hospital in Avicenne . . . bacteria aren't stupid. They don't want to be treated in a Moroccan hospital. They waited until I was in Sweden to show up. Here in Stockholm I can see a doctor, any doctor, with complete confidence. You know, when I'm on vacation down there, I avoid even aspirin. The medicines there always contain less than the prescribed dosage. Watch out for anything written in Arabic. Do you think that if it says a thousand units of penicillin there really are a thousand? They put in three or four hundred and write one thousand. I have proof. At the beginning I took Moroccan drugs. There was no ef-

fect, nothing. They don't work. They are crap, you understand? Such a beautiful country, and such shitty medicine! In
this magnificent country, you find real Muslims. I mean
Swedes who are really Protestant or Catholic, but they treat
us as if they were Muslims. They are kind and generous, with
a sense of solidarity. This country deserves to be Muslim.
No, I don't mean fundamentalist. That's not Islam. That's
political crap. In fact, the poor Swedes are afraid that Muslim fanatics will come here and ruin their nice peaceful country, and I can understand that. Tell me, how do you feel?
Here, I guarantee you, you'll get better. In this country, they
don't make a distinction between rich and poor, between
Swedes and immigrants; everyone is treated the same, and I
admire that. I say this because some of our fellow Moroccans
are never satisfied, they complain, make a lot of noise, drink,
and behave badly. They don't respect this country, and that's
not good!"

I liked this guy's face. He reminded me of a camel. He was
tall, with long arms. For all his babbling, I had no idea what
he was suffering from. He was trying to be positive, but he
spouted all kinds of garbage. It's not true that the medicine is
less strong than the prescription says in Morocco. These were
his biases, that's all. I would have liked to have this man's energy, his faith in progress, his passion for this cold country. I
had too many doubts, another characteristic I shared with my
friend Ali. It was that, more than anything else, which had

brought us so close. I told myself I should stop comparing these two countries. They did not have the same history, climate, or fate. Even if Swedish medicine was remarkable, I wanted to go home to Morocco. How could I explain this need, this burning sensation, this clog that blocked everything in my chest? Before talking to Lovgren about this, or even to my wife, I called Ali. I didn't tell him I was sick; certainly not. I didn't want to worry him, to plunge him into despair. All I said was that I missed the wind from the east, I missed the dust of Tangier. He said he would send me some!

Two weeks later, two packages arrived from Ali. One was a hermetically sealed plastic bottle, labeled EAST WIND FROM TANGIER, APRIL 13, 1990. In the other was a small metal box full of gray powder: TANGIER DUST. He also sent fabric swatches for the curtains in our apartment. He continued to be busy with the decoration and remodeling. My heart was no longer in it. I needed good health, not curtains.

I continued to work, without slowing down much. I finally told my wife, who didn't say a word for twenty-four hours. She was unable to speak. She was distraught, defeated, pacing from room to room in our house. She hid, so she could cry alone. She called Dr. Lovgren, who reassured her. "We'll fight this together," he told her. She rallied. "We can't let this damn thing get the better of us, destroying our marriage and our life together," she said. "We have the means to fight this. We will stay in this country and conquer it."

She was strong. I held her in my arms with a feeling I had never experienced before. Our love had to be stronger than the disease.

15

I MADE UP MY MIND. Ali would know nothing about my sickness. Moreover, Ali could no longer be my friend. The knowledge would destroy him, make him suffer. I did not need his suffering. The rupture between us would surprise him, but it would hurt him less in the long run. His friendship was too precious for me to abandon it to unhappiness, despair at the mercy of the interminable process of cell destruction. One thing was certain. I would never see his tortured face approach mine for a final good-bye. I would never see those eyes, filled with tears and memories, leaving me. Above all, I would not have to read my own distress on his face, a face so transparent that it could become cruel. If I survived, I would explain everything to him. If I disappeared, he would receive a letter after I died.

I thought about telling Ramon. He was like a brother, and I always had a good time with him. I needed levity, laughter, lightness. With Ramon, all of that was possible. Our relationship was not deep enough for him to become teary and melodramatic. I liked Ramon. He had converted to Islam for love! I had to stage a breakup with Ali, pick a fight to ruin everything. What destroys a close friendship? Betrayal. But Ali did not have a seed of treachery in him. It would be total injustice to accuse him of being a traitor. If he had it in him to betray me, he would have done so on other occasions. Breach of trust? He was incapable of that, too. I found myself walking down a boulevard under a cold sun, considering different scenarios to protect our friendship from the tragedy of death. I was torn between the idea of a complete break, with no explanation, no words, and a carefully planned argument.

I discovered within myself a capacity for perversion, a diabolical imagination and a sick pleasure in toying with the emotions of the people I loved. This distracted me. I staged my illness like a play. I was giving out parts. In the muted Scandinavian light, I was playing with peoples' lives. I was no longer a Moroccan lost in a country that was too civilized; I was no longer a doctor serving the poorest countries of the world; I was no longer the attentive and generous friend; I was in the process of extending my hand to the devil. Was I doing it out of an excess of goodness? It was more likely weakness, cruelty, selfishness. I walked along, talking to myself. No one looked at me. You can talk to yourself without being perceived as insane. In Morocco, when people go out into the streets, screaming in distress and rending their clothes, nobody pays attention. People assume they have lost everything, except their sanity. For us, they are almost saints, touched by divine grace.

I was refining my plans when I heard a deep and serious voice. I turned around. There was no one there. The voice continued. "You are losing your mind. What is this all about, this idea of sparing your friend, but hurting him terribly? Where did you get this idea? Film noir? Or maybe that movie about jealousy in which a woman persecutes her husband even after he dies, planting evidence that he tried to killed her?" I think it was *Mortal Sin* with Gene Tierney. It was complicated and terrifying. "No, my friend. Worry about your illness. Take care of yourself. Get better. Let your friends comfort you; let them help you through these hard times. You have no right to be cruel to someone you love, someone with whom you have shared good times and bad. It's some kind of jealousy deep in your soul, expressing itself in a perverse, cynical way. Jealousy is human. It's unfair, but commonplace. Jealousy has nothing to do with reason. Why be jealous of Ali? What does he have that you don't? His health! The most precious of all gifts! He will survive you, he will continue to live out your friendship in sorrow. Then life will take over. He won't forget you, perhaps, but absence and silence will create an eternal distance between you. Sickness has brought out the dark side of your soul. You're listening to it as you plan this diabolical scheme. No, I refuse to believe you are capable of this."

The voice spoke to me and then was gone. I recalled scenes from the movie Ali liked so much. I remembered when the woman let her young handicapped brother-in-law drown in icy water because her husband spent too much time taking care of him. I remember the poison she gave her sister, before hiding the bottle in the sister's room, because she was jealous of her. I remember the way she wrapped her feet in a rug and deliberately fell down the stairs in order to lose the baby she was carrying. She was already jealous of the baby. I still remember how much this film disturbed me. But why was I thinking about this? I wasn't going to kill anyone. I was just ending a friendship that had lasted too long, in order to confront the pain of my illness alone. My reasons weren't clear. That's illness for you. Death itself is nothing. The real death is sickness, the long and painful sickness.

Another voice encouraged me. We are all contradictory, ambivalent, irrational. I coughed, I was tired, and I wanted to cry. When she came home, Ghita had red eyes. She must have been crying. The children were sleeping. I kissed them without waking them up. I refused to let myself break down. I had to keep up my morale. The next morning I had my first chemotherapy session.

16

I NO LONGER RESPONDED to Ali's letters. When he called, Ghita told him I was on a mission in Africa or Asia. His last letters expressed alarm. He didn't understand what was going on, but he thought that something had happened and wanted to understand. I maintained my silence. When he told my wife that he was very worried, that he was getting ready to come see me because he suspected serious illness (I think he meant depression), I took the phone and spoke to him, my tone cold and dry. "No," I told him, "there's no point in you coming here. I'm coming to Tangier. I just have to finish some business here, and then I'll come. You prepare the bills, and we'll settle our accounts." I hung up without allowing him to respond. I was playing my role. I felt strong. It was curious, the extent to which provoking this dispute with Ali was boosting my energy. I didn't make any effort to speak to him. It was as if he had become an enemy.

My wife didn't understand this cruel charade. I was incapable of explaining my deepest feelings to her, or the reasons for my behavior. She did not like conflict in relationships. I made up something, saying Ali had disappointed me. She believed this immediately, adding her own examples of his supposed hypocrisy, which troubled me and made me feel worse. "Yes, now you get it. Your friend takes advantage of you. He's a profiteer, like everybody else in whom you confided without ever asking yourself why they were interested in you. People are jealous and hypocritical. Ali's no exception. Like the man who sold you your car after rigging the odometer. Like the man at the ministry in Morocco who said he was your friend, and then reported on you to the authorities before you left for Sweden. You're surrounded by people who put obstacles in your path. You had to come to Sweden to realize that. Ali might be nice enough, but his wife isn't—she's jealous of you, me, our children. It's natural she'd be jealous, since she can't have children of her own. Forget them all. Concentrate on getting your health back."

I didn't have the strength to answer Ghita. I was trapped. "You're wrong," I wanted to say, "but you'll understand later. Please don't speak badly of others, especially not Ali. We have thirty years of friendship behind us. Please respect this, and let me work things out in my own way."

I began to have doubts. I had set a dangerous spiral of evil in motion. I needed to keep Ghita out of it. But how? How could I convince her that this didn't concern her? I needed to turn her into a neutral bystander who would ignore my behavior toward Ali. Her hardness had always taken me aback. Beneath her angelic appearance was a woman of steel, without compassion or compromise. Where did it come from? Her childhood, most likely. She had lived with her mother in the Rif Mountains. Her father had gone to work in Germany, and he returned once every two years, in the summers. She was raised without joy or affection. But she always refused to seek help. She said she was not interested in changing her behavior or her temperament. Ghita never expressed doubts. She was always sure of herself. It was almost impossible to negotiate with her. Fortunately, she had her good points. Sincere and frank, she could not stand the social hypocrisy so widespread in Morocco. She was remarkably intelligent, and made sure our children were getting a good education. She was both soft and hard.

17

SIX MONTHS AFTER my first chemotherapy session, Dr. Lovgren became more optimistic, saying I could travel. He said I could go to Morocco on vacation, but I had to be careful, I could never touch another cigarette, and I should not even sit next to a smoker, or in a smoky room. That was going to be difficult in a country where everybody smoked.

Whether it was an opinion I had formed before seeing it, a self-fulfilling prophecy, or bad faith, I did not like the way Ali had furnished the apartment. That was a good enough pretext for a dispute. I waited for the right moment. As always, Ali was generous and helpful. He told me I had lost weight, that I looked different. I told him it was my work, the constant travel, and disappointment in married life. We had coffee together, and he confided in me, just like in the old days. He talked about his Spanish mistress, a nymphomaniac. "It's sex, it's all about sex, no feelings or emotions," he said. "She's obsessed with sex." He added: "I don't feel guilty, since she's not a threat to my marriage, or to my emotional life."

I was suddenly jealous. I wanted something like this to tell him. In marrying Ghita, I had opted for marital fidelity, never looking at other women. It was a rational and comfortable decision. It tested my willpower. I loved Ghita. I could have had an affair with Dr. Lovgren's assistant. Briggit was available, and she made it clear to me in various ways, but I resisted. I had an impulse to tell Ali that he stereotyped women as either sexually obsessed or hysterical, but that wasn't really true of him. I did not want to pursue this discussion. I needed to set the stage for our forthcoming conflict. I asked him what he thought of *Mortal Sin.* He was astounded. It was overdone, he said. The screenplay was good, and so was the acting, but it was extreme. This wasn't jealousy; this was pathological. I asked what he thought about substituting a friendship between two men for the relationship between husband and wife. He had no idea what I was getting at. "There's no room for jealousy in a friendship," he said. "Friendship is pure; it's not based on sexual or material interest." He added: "You know, since you moved to Sweden, your attitude has changed. Has there ever been jealousy between us? I don't think so. We're friends because we share certain values and interests. We help each other, we have faced ordeals together, we know we can count on each other, there are no issues with women or money between us. What are you getting at, Mamed?"

I could have launched into the argument right then and there, but I was a coward. I looked at him with tears in my eyes. I wanted to cry for myself, my plight, the things I was setting in motion. I bowed my head to avoid showing my feelings. I backed out of the dinner he had prepared for us that night. I said it was fatigue and malaise. Ali offered to come and keep me company. I discouraged him, and promised we would see each other the next day.

Ghita told me again that Ali's wife was jealous. "I don't like the way she looks at our children. She can't stand the idea of not having any of her own, even if Nabil is so cute," she said. "You don't think so? You think I'm wrong? You should trust my intuition. This friend of yours, the one you're always putting on a pedestal . . ." I told her to stop. I would not allow her to judge thirty years of friendship. It was not her problem. She needed to show some respect.

Ghita's comments upset me and I couldn't sleep. I put off the confrontation with Ali. I don't know why, but I wanted to let Ramon know what was going on. I called him, and we talked for a long time. He listened without saying anything.

When we got back to Stockholm, I slept for two days straight. The fatigue, the grief, the sorrow, the feeling of having made an irreparable mistake, all that in the midst of my illness. I was completely confused. Everything was mixed up—good and evil, goodwill and guilt, the stench of jealousy, and the genuine desire to spare my friend my anguish. The certainty of approaching "the dark void," as my grandfather called it, preoccupied me night and day. I became obsessed with the damp ground in which my body would lie forever. Everything brought me back to this devastating thought.

I received several letters from Ali. I forced myself to answer them brusquely, without emotion. I turned this page of my life painfully, and at the same time wondered whether it had been a good idea. To calm my nerves, I drafted my posthumous letter to Ali.

III

Ramon

THREE YEARS LATER

A long-standing witness to this friendship, I found myself involved in its dissolution. I refused to pass judgment on this sad affair. Mamed told me his version of the story. Ali did the same. I understood that it was not simply a question of differing points of view.

Ravaged by illness, told by the doctors that his condition was terminal, Mamed decided to return to his country to die. He called me the day before he arrived, and asked me not to tell anyone. I met him and his wife and children at the airport. His withered face was stark testimony to the advanced disease. They moved into Mamed's parents' old house. He slept in his mother's bed, and stopped taking the medicine Dr. Lovgren had said was useless at this point. He closed his eyes and waited for death to take him. In Morocco, we say that you can see death in a person's eyes forty days before it comes. Ghita was distraught, but she managed to appear strong. She told her children Swedish fairy tales to prepare them for the loss and void ahead. I went to see Mamed twice a day. I told Ghita I would do the shopping and take care of the children.

As soon as Mamed learned that his case was hopeless, he had a passionate desire to leave Sweden in order to die in the family home. He believed Moroccan soil was better suited to the dead than the glacial soil of Scandinavia. He no longer had the energy to compare the two countries, to criticize everything that didn't work in Morocco. He wanted to stand once more on the soil of the country he carried in his heart.

His parents' house was in a state of terrible disrepair. His father lived there alone, surrounded by his history books and an address book in which many of the names had been crossed out. An old peasant woman came to clean once in a while. The old man said nothing, waiting for the end of his days with the faith of a good Muslim who had already put his life in Allah's hands. He forgot to take his medicine, convinced that everything was already determined in heaven, and that after a lifetime of reading, now it was time for prayer.

Seeing his son was a shock. He was confronted with a man who looked as old as he was. He wept silently, citing a verse of the Koran that says everything happens according to Allah's will. Despite their suffering, different in intensity, father and son felt a need to communicate. I knew Mamed did not have a religious bone in his body. When he was fifteen, he would sneak out of the house to eat during Ramadan, either at Ali's house or mine. He did believe in some kind of higher spirituality, and he liked Islamic mystic poetry, especially by Sufi Ibn Arabi. I stayed there, trying to make myself scarce, witnessing this final coming together of father and son. When I got up to leave, Mamed signaled me to stay.

Mamed's father believed that the mystics made the divine spirit into an idol, which some even dared confuse with Allah. Mamed did not contradict him, and enjoyed their conversations. They realized that they had rarely had the opportunity to talk to each other. "How are you, my son?" his father asked. "I don't mean your health, which is in Allah's hands, but in general. How was life in Sweden? You know, I wanted to visit you there. I used to dream about Scandinavia. For me, it represented honesty, social justice, democracy. But maybe I'm wrong. Some people hold up Britain as an example, but a country that colonized other countries can never be an example for others. You know, my son, I was tempted to get involved in politics when Morocco became independent, but I quickly realized we weren't ready for democracy. Not that we didn't deserve it, but we needed to be taught what democracy is. We had to learn to live together. Democracy is not simply a question of putting your ballot in a ballot box. It takes time. It's a culture that needs to be learned.

"How are things with your wife?" he went on. "No problems, I hope? Well, everybody has them, of course. I can tell
you want to rest now. If you don't mind, I'll read some verses
from the Koran so you'll sleep peacefully. Afterward, we can
listen to some music. I know you like Mozart, don't you?
Mozart couldn't have been Moroccan. The proof is that we
have no one of his caliber."

He sat on the edge of his son's bed, watching him and
reading the Koran. Then he prayed silently. Mamed fell
asleep, forgetting the music. I prayed, too.

Mamed slept badly, thrashing around as if fighting
demons in a nightmare. He was struggling against death,
which was fast approaching him with open arms.

Ghita divided her time between her husband and her children. Most of the time, she had to leave the children with a
cousin who ran a private school. She answered the telephone,
and politely refused most visitors. "Mamed is tired. As soon
as he feels better, he'll come to visit you." When Ali called,
Ghita paused, hesitated, looked at me, then went and whispered in her husband's ear. Then she spoke into the phone:
"I'm sorry, Ali," she said. "He doesn't want to see anyone. It's
best to respect his wishes. If he saw you, it might make him
worse. Good-bye." She looked at me again, as if to make me
an accomplice. I lowered my eyes, as if I hadn't understood
what she had said.

I imagined Ali, tears in his eyes, a look of defeat on his

face, despair in his heart. He must have been thinking: "But this is when he needs me. This is the most important moment in our friendship, whatever differences and misunderstandings we've had. I have to see him. I must tell him that my love is sincere, pure, even if he was mistaken about me, even if his wife did everything in her power to separate us. At the same time, I know him. When he's sick, he doesn't want anyone to see him. I remember when he got sick in the disciplinary camp, he asked me to turn out the light, so people couldn't see his tired face, wracked with fever. Today, it's much more serious. If he came home to Morocco, it's because there is no more hope. I absolutely must see him, unless . . . maybe it's better this way. Perhaps he wants me to preserve the image of a lively, happy Mamed, at peace with himself. Or maybe he's angry with me. But why? Because I will outlive him? Could it be that simple? No, Mamed isn't like that. I can't believe it."

I did not find it hard to put myself in Ali's place, to imagine what he must have felt. I saw him struggling with the suspicions running through his mind, questioning himself. Something had happened, but what? He admitted that he searched constantly for the root of the misunderstanding: a careless word, an inappropriate gesture, a joke in poor taste, a lack of attention, some failure on his part. He continually replayed the last few years of their relationship. There had been no obvious drama, mishap, or misunderstanding. Their friendship had been open and transparent. They told each other everything, confided their secrets in each other. So why this harsh about-face? I think they did not have the same perception of things, that clear divergences existed, but they never brought them up. The story about the apartment was just a pretext. Mamed's wife could never have influenced him to that extent.

Ali had spent three years pondering the cause of this inexplicable breakup. The way he explained it to himself was that Mamed had changed. Time and distance might have played their role in the wear and tear on their relationship. He clung to the image of his friend as a man of his word, a faithful friend, but decided that Mamed had taken another path in life, discovered new horizons, and didn't want to be bound by a relationship that reminded him of his youth and adolescence. Maybe he thought of their friendship as a book he had read too many times. Now it was time to start a new one.

Each time, Ali found the beginning of an explanation but was unable to follow it to the end of the argument. He had heard a story about two Egyptian friends, writers who had chosen to use the same pseudonym. They were so inseparable that people called them twins. They were different but melded together by a bond that had been severely tested in Nasser's political prisons. When they married, they managed to persuade their spouses that their friendship was sacred, even more important than their conjugal lives. But the Egyptians' story was an exception. The reason they were used as examples was that complete harmony reigned between their families.

Whenever Mamed felt well enough, he worked on his posthumous letter to Ali. As soon as his wife was away and his father was asleep, he wrote. This letter was immensely important to him. Even his illness was eclipsed while he wrote to his friend. When he was writing, he felt better. His ideas were clear. Two doctor friends came to see him from time to time, and told funny stories to cheer him up. They left as soon as they saw that he was tired. They were the jokers among his old gang at medical school. They loved risqué stories, and they never ran out of steamy gossip. I no longer felt like telling jokes. I was at Mamed's disposal. I spent hours with him. I didn't ask him anything; I read crime fiction. I kept thinking about this friendship that was ending in drama, and I realized that I had never had a close friend.

One morning, Mamed asked Ghita to bring the children to see him. Ghita called me. It was a Monday in winter, and the sun was shining.

Mamed wanted to speak to the children. Yanis and Adil were conscious of the gravity of the occasion. They held each other's hands, not allowing themselves to cry. "Come here, so I can kiss you both. Stick together no matter what. Take care of each other. Life is beautiful, life awaits you. Be confident, and generous. Do not humiliate or bring shame on anyone. Stick up for yourselves. Go now. Be happy!"

Ghita cried. Mamed put his hands on her eyes. Night entered his room, never to leave it.

Mamed was buried in the cemetery of the Mujahideen, the freedom fighters. It was a simple grave, under a tree. Ali was among the crowd of mourners, one man among many others. His sorrow was immense. He felt alone. I decided not to disturb him.

IV

The Letter

Ali,

I have been carrying this letter within me for years. I have read it and reread it, without actually writing it. From the day when I first grasped the seriousness of my illness, I wanted to spare you. You will find my attitude strange, and probably unfair. It took us more than thirty years to construct our friendship, and I did not want sickness, suffering, and unhappiness to destroy it. You see, I'm your friend, and I did for you what I would have liked you to do for me, had a fatal illness had the temerity to attack you.

I had this idea when I was at my lowest, at a time when I had not yet realized that death is part of life, and that when we leave life, we should not punish those who survive us. I knew better than most that death is really the illness, not the actual moment when everything stops. What is death? The long days, the interminable nights of insomnia, when pain bores its mark into your body until you lose consciousness. The hours waiting in a hospital room until someone calls you for an examination. Death is the test results, the numbers, the speculation about the unknown. Death is the silence, the frightening abyss we watch approaching us.

I could not spare my wife and children this grief. But I could spare you, simply by provoking an argument, by questioning your honesty, which I knew to be your most sensitive point. I needed to push you away, to cast you aside, with your suspicions, your questions, your extreme sensitivity, your sense of injustice. By detaching you from our friendship, I was pushing you away from my death, hoping you could turn the page.

I suspected that this strategy would not work as well as I had planned. I had foreseen that you would resist, that you would try to find out what was really happening, and do everything you could to understand the torment in your heart. I knew you were deeply hurt, and that you would not give up easily. This is precisely what I feared. Your intelligence and the strength of your conviction could make my plan fail. Above all, I wanted to avoid having to share my death with you, because I know what you are like. You would have been there, living through every moment of the progression of this damn disease; you would have been at my side, waiting with me to the end; and I would have had to read the approach of the darkness in your eyes. You were a mirror I could not bear to look into, out of weakness, wounded pride, and, I have to confess, perhaps out of a terrible jealousy unworthy of our friendship. Your face would have been there between sickness and death, at the frontier of the abyss. I would have seen the beginning of the end in your eyes. Do you remember that Humphrey Bogart film? You're the one who explained to me that the "Big Sleep" is death, and because of this, the film was unintelligible, although it was superb.

Now I am lying in a bed that is slowly turning into a tomb, and I know you are right.

Together we shared intense moments, especially when we were in the hands of the imbecile military officials, who spoke bad French, because they could not speak to us any other way, and that was all part of the humiliation their superiors wanted to inflict on us. You were strong because you understood and refused to submit. We complemented each other. I had a big mouth. I knew how to talk back, to fight if necessary. You withstood blows, too, but you weren't able to return them. You were the cerebral one; I was the physical one. Actually, I was both, but in these circumstances, I preferred to flex my muscle. We were dealing with brutes, who understood only the language of brutes.

Our friendship has been a beautiful journey. Neither of us has ever done anything petty, unworthy, or mediocre. We took great care in our relationship, cultivating our friendship openly, without ambiguity, without lies. When our wives appeared, there was a moment when we wavered, but we both hung on. They had a hard time accepting the strength of our friendship. There were some crises. They could never understand that our bond could sometimes be stronger than the bond we felt with our families. Jealousy is a banal sentiment, but normal. We just need to understand it, and not be surprised when it bursts into flame.

I missed you a lot, especially in my first years in Sweden. I wanted to show you that country, share with you my daily life there, discuss the Swedish way of life with you, their cold rationality, their great kindness, their culture of respect for one another—in short, what was lacking in our own beloved country.

I learned the language, and I was proud to be able to watch Bergman films without subtitles. I took advantage of Sweden's location to visit neighboring countries. I had a particular fondness for Denmark. Everywhere I went, I encountered fellow Moroccans, some of whom were lost souls, others political exiles, still others who had simply come to work and make their lives in that part of the world. They all told me the same thing. They missed Morocco, even if they had suffered there. It's strange, this strong, neurotic relationship we have with our homeland. I needed to come back here to die.

Perhaps it's because of our cemeteries. The tombs are arranged any which way. No one minds the chaos. Children offer to water the grass on the tomb you have come to visit. Old peasants read verses from the Koran so quickly that they swallow half their words, in order to make ten dirhams from a mourner. Our cemeteries are part of nature. They are not sad places. If you could see the one in Stockholm! Sterile, orderly, depressing. Of course, many Scandinavians choose to be cremated. Muslims don't do that. To be reduced to a little pile of ashes, put in a box, then scattered to the wind— how romantic! To think that we return to the earth to fertilize it, and become reincarnated in a plant or a flower. We never talked about this. Do you remember when you went through your atheist phase? You told me you would try to give your children tree or flower names, instead of Islamic ones. You rejected any religious references. After a while, you let go of this rigidity. You replaced it with another: you didn't accept social hypocrisy. We agreed on what was essential. You made me laugh because you searched for perfection in people. You didn't say it quite that way, but you were surprised when someone didn't keep his word, or when you caught someone in a lie.

I liked your relationship with women. I had settled down. I nurtured my relationship with the beautiful Ghita. I no longer seduced other women. But women were your weakness. An evening without a woman was a failure. A trip wasn't memorable unless you met a new woman. I was astonished when you told me you were getting married. You wanted to join the ranks of married men to be like me, to have both the stability and tensions of married life. We both had marital problems. Neither of our wives ever really accepted our friendship. We stole from them time we should have been spending with them. What you and I shared was spiritual. With our wives, it was sensual above all else.

Thirty years with some eclipses, some moments of silence, some separation due to travel. There were moments that gave us pause, but there were never any doubts. We never called our friendship into question. We always met again with the same gaze, the same strong sense of each other. People thought we agreed on everything. In fact, what gave depth to our relationship was precisely the opposite: it was our different perspectives, our differences of opinion, freely expressed, but without any kind of personal opposition between us. We complemented each other and defended the force that cemented our bond.

I have found our rupture hard to endure. Many times, I almost flew back to Tangier to tell you what I had done. I never had the courage, and then it was too late. I believed in my decision, and I couldn't take it back. When I seemed to be angry with you, talking about the bills for the apartment, I worked hard to be believable, using all my talents as an actor to pull it off. I needed the strength of my conviction.

Now, I return to you your due. Our friendship was a great and beautiful adventure. It does not end with my death. It remains a part of the life you will continue to live.

Mohammed
Tangier, Morocco, July 2003–January 2004

FOR MORE TAHAR BEN JELLOUN, LOOK FOR THE

This Blinding Absence of Light

An immediate and critically acclaimed bestseller in France, *This Blinding Absence of Light* is the latest work by internationally renowned author Tahar Ben Jelloun, the first North African winner of the Prix Goncourt and winner of the Prix Mahgreb. Crafting real life events into narrative fiction, Ben Jelloun reveals the horrific story of the desert concentration camps where King Hassan II of Morocco held his political enemies in underground cells with no light and only enough food and water to keep them lingering on the edge of death. After working closely with one of the survivors, Ben Jelloun has written a story in the simplest of language and delivers a shocking novel that explores both the depths of inhumanity and the unbelievable endurance of the human will.

"In this deeply moving novel, Tahar Ben Jelloun has chosen imagination as the response to inhumanity—the art of writing as the ultimate liberation."

—*L'Express*

ISBN: 978-0-14-303572-5

FOR THE BEST IN PAPERBACKS, LOOK FOR THE

In every corner of the world, on every subject under the sun, Penguin represents quality and variety—the very best in publishing today.

For complete information about books available from Penguin—including Penguin Classics and Puffins—and how to order them, write to us at the appropriate address below. Please note that for copyright reasons the selection of books varies from country to country.

In the United States: Please write to *Penguin Group (USA), P.O. Box 12289 Dept. B, Newark, New Jersey 07101-5289* or call 1-800-788-6262.

In the United Kingdom: Please write to *Dept. EP, Penguin Books Ltd, Bath Road, Harmondsworth, West Drayton, Middlesex UB7 0DA.*

In Canada: Please write to *Penguin Books Canada Ltd, 90 Eglinton Avenue East, Suite 700, Toronto, Ontario M4P 2Y3.*

In Australia: Please write to *Penguin Books Australia Ltd, P.O. Box 257, Ringwood, Victoria 3134.*

In New Zealand: Please write to *Penguin Books (NZ) Ltd, Private Bag 102902, North Shore Mail Centre, Auckland 10.*

In India: Please write to *Penguin Books India Pvt Ltd, 11 Panchsheel Shopping Centre, Panchsheel Park, New Delhi 110 017.*

In the Netherlands: Please write to *Penguin Books Netherlands bv, Postbus 3507, NL-1001 AH Amsterdam.*

In Germany: Please write to *Penguin Books Deutschland GmbH, Metzlerstrasse 26, 60594 Frankfurt am Main.*

In Spain: Please write to *Penguin Books S. A., Bravo Murillo 19, 1° B, 28015 Madrid.*

In Italy: Please write to *Penguin Italia s.r.l., Via Benedetto Croce 2, 20094 Corsico, Milano.*

In France: Please write to *Penguin France, Le Carré Wilson, 62 rue Benjamin Baillaud, 31500 Toulouse.*

In Japan: Please write to *Penguin Books Japan Ltd, Kaneko Building, 2-3-25 Koraku, Bunkyo-Ku, Tokyo 112.*

In South Africa: Please write to *Penguin Books South Africa (Pty) Ltd, Private Bag X14, Parkview, 2122 Johannesburg.*